The Search for Susu

The Search for Susu

Book 1 in the
Scandal in Academe Series

T.M. Giggetts
Marcella McCoy-Deh

The Search for Susu

ISBN: 978-0-692-51698-0

NewSeason Books
PO Box 1403
Havertown, PA 19083
www.newseasonbooks.com
newseasonbooks@gmail.com

Prologue

The man, with his thick matted hair and disheveled clothes, lay unmoving on the floor of the one room flat. A thin line of blood streaked from his forehead, down the side of his face, eventually pooling behind his neck on the floor. The boy put his right hand on the leg of the man—his left still holding the gravedigger's shovel—and shook him fiercely.

"No, no, no, nooo! Please wake up, Sir. Please!"

Suddenly a terrible shriek filled the already humid, Montserrat air. The girl, with her torn dress and wet face, cried and waved her hands wildly. It wasn't the dead body on the floor that birthed her travail. It was the woman across the room whose eyes had begun to roll into the back of her head.

The teenagers darted over to the dining table where the woman sat, teacup barely dangling from her index finger. Her head tilted back in an odd angle as she slowly slid from the chair.

The boy caught the thick woman before she crashed onto the floor. He laid her gently on her side.

The girl looked back and forth between the boy with the shovel and the woman who'd begun gasping, choking, and vomiting onto the rotting wood floor.

What had they done?

The boy's eyes reflected the panic in her own. They had no idea what to do.

Abruptly, the woman, nightgown drenched in sweat or tears or something else entirely, called out to the girl, her words unintelligible.

The girl leaned down, not caring that the hem of her dress was soaked with vomit. She grabbed the woman's swollen arm just as it went limp and flopped onto the floor.

"We must go!" The boy whispered despite them being the only two people alive in the room.

Shock blanketed the face of the girl.

What had they done?

"We will go down to the Shoppes and ask for help, OK? We will say she took ill, OK?"

He said this as he slowly unraveled the girl's hand from around the wilted appendage, a severance that seemed to awaken her sorrow.

She wailed uncontrollably.

"Mommy?! Oh Mommyyyyyyyy!!!"

The boy, massive tears welling in his eyes, held the girl close, turning her face into the place where his shoulder and chest met.

"Shhh. It's alright, Love. I will take care of you. I will always take care of you. God help us."

The girl looked up at him; her eyes were red and glazed. His face was resolute even if she was sure his mind was racing with uncertainty. With the blood and excrement of two dead people beneath their feet, she wasn't sure if they could survive the weight of it all—much less the shame.

1

"You're cute. But let's see what you look like with your clothes off."

The bug-eyed woman with stringy, dirty blond hair waved her hand toward a set of lockers. Francine balked at the order despite knowing full well that when she answered the ad, she also agreed to comply with such a request.

"What do you mean?" Francine asked, feigning as much innocence as she could muster.

The woman smirked. She was used to the stalling of the young ones.

She chuckled and said, "I have the perfect slippers for those cold feet of yours."

Francine briefly looked away from the woman. Not quite in shame. Shame-ish.

"You want to be a dancer, right?" the woman continued.

Francine hedged. "Well actually, I was hoping I could be a waitress first. You know, just until I got used to everything."

Bug Eyes clipped her pen onto the clipboard she'd just picked up in anticipation of evaluating Francine's body and moves.

"We don't have any waitressing positions open. It's either dancing or nothing."

Francine stared back at the woman. *I have to draw the line somewhere*, she thought.

And this was her line. She'd find another way to make money. Another way to shrink the stack of bills that were collecting on her desk. Another way to tackle the mountainous loan debt she'd accumulated while completing her graduate degrees.

"I'm sorry. I've made a mistake," Francine said.

The woman nodded her head. "Uh huh."

She'd seen it all before. Young girls excited about the $500 a day the ad said they could make dancing. Once they arrived at the stark, dark-grey building isolated on the industrial end of Delaware Avenue, and it's confirmed that they would actually have to dance nude, they often decided the money wasn't worth it. And from what Bug Eyes knew from her 15 years of managing *Johnny's Joint*, it wasn't. But that wasn't a fact she was inclined to share.

"Alright, sweets. Thanks for coming by." The woman turned away and began barking orders to the large, bulky men who were setting up the club for opening.

Francine picked up her bag, walked out through the large iron double doors, and quickly headed to her car. After putting the key in the ignition, the car sputtered and spit before engaging the engine—another sign of her dire financial circumstances and where she didn't want to be in her life.

She laid her head on the steering wheel and released her tears. She had to do something.

***

Ravencrest College took its landscaping cues from the rolling hills and countryside of England, the homeland of its founders. With manicured lawns, bushes shaped and pruned within an inch of their vegetative lives, and stunning stone architecture, the private, liberal arts college sat adjacent to a large dairy farm just northeast of the city of Philadelphia. The campus of 7,500 students reeked with privilege and peace, an especially odd combination of merits since this is where the peaceless Francine spent most of her days as an adjunct professor in the Department of Humanities and Social Sciences.

Sitting in the adjunct office grading papers, Francine wondered aloud, "Do students just write stuff to piss us off or are they really just that ill-equipped to think critically about a subject—any subject, really?"

The two other professors in the office nodded in solidarity with the frustration at the core of her rhetorical question. No need for an answer. They'd all found themselves venting a time or two in the safety of those four walls; in the tight office that served as their office/lounge.

Agatha, an older woman with pale skin and salt-and-pepper hair styled and feathered a la Dorothy from the Golden Girls, stood up and began packing her bag. She turned to Francine.

"You look down, Fran. What's up?"

She walked over to Francine and sat next to her on the aged brown leather couch.

"Eh." Francine shrugged and continued grading.

"Oh, I know that sound. That's the sound of someone who just got paid."

They both looked at each other knowingly. This made Francine laugh. She laughed long and hard and deep, and Agatha joined her. It was good to know she wasn't the only one struggling.

"Well, look at it like this," Agatha said. "At least you don't have to go down here to the damn food stamp office and wait for hours for them to call your name, just so you can get a little help feeding the grandchild that your no-count son left with you."

Francine stopped laughing. The other professor in the room stood up quickly and began packing his messenger bag. As he left, his face was red and his eyes still bulged at Agatha's confession. His quick departure was not lost on the old woman.

She waved her hand. "Pshh! I've long stopped caring about what other people think."

"So wait … you get food stamps? A card?" Francine asked. She was shocked.

"I know, I know. I'm a white woman of a certain age. I drive a late-model Lexus and teach at one of the top schools in the region. Doesn't make sense, huh?"

Francine didn't know what to make of Agatha's mentioning of her own race. As if to say that typically her food-stamp situation should be the plight of someone else. Someone of color. Certainly not her because, well, she's white. But after three years of teaching at the college, Francine had become almost immune to the daily well-intentioned, micro-aggressions she experienced from students, staff, and faculty alike. Almost.

Nevertheless, she let this one pass only because she wanted to hear more.

"So, you have to wait?"

"Yep," Agatha continued. "Every quarter they evaluate my situation, and every quarter I have to go back and tell them, 'no, the union has not been able to negotiate a higher per-credit hour salary for adjuncts' and 'no, it doesn't look like that's going to happen next year' and 'no, my workload doesn't allow for me to pick up a part-time job.'"

At this point, Agatha looked like she was fighting back tears. Francine didn't know what to do. They weren't close—not even friends really—but she could feel the woman's pain. It was familiar.

"Well, maybe a full-time position will open up soon." These were the only words that Francine could think of to help. They were the words she would have wanted to hear.

"Nope. I've given up on that race," Agatha said, the fire back in her voice. "I'm an English professor. And an old one, at that. Do you know how many people are vying for full-time English positions?"

Francine *didn't* know but didn't want to say she didn't know.

"Too many," Agatha answered.

"So, I'm going to either leave higher ed altogether or just stick it out as the proverbial stepchild I am. We'll see."

She stood up and grabbed her bag. "Let me get out of here, I have class in a few minutes. You'll be okay, you know. Whatever's going on."

After the woman left, Francine pulled out her journal; the one she kept with her for the book she hoped to write some day.

That will never be me, she writes.

***

One of the reasons why Francine was determined to not let her colleague's plight become her own—why she would never apply for food stamps no matter how much she could use it—was because of her family. She was afraid she'd be letting them down if they ever found out how far she'd fallen. Especially her father. They all were so proud of her. *He* was so proud of her for following her passion, especially when so many of her peers followed the proscribed paths of their ilk: whatever pursuits would continue to build the family's coffers and reputations. Her parents often said they worked hard and smart to invest in the dreams of their children.

"Your generation is the first to live your dreams without the class and race restrictions. Ours is the first to realize the dream of seeing our children's hearts really soar. *Pursue your passion*!" he would toast at her graduation celebration.

She was DOCTOR Francine Marie Carty, professor of cultural studies with a specialty in Africana studies and literature at the prestigious Ravencrest College. Sure, they didn't like that she was still working as an "adjunct" professor instead of a full time, preferably, tenure track appointment. Still, the baby of the family had become a doctor and might someday distinguish herself in her field.

Francine came from a middle-class, Caribbean family with a strong work ethic. The Cartys owned and operated a very successful funeral service in southern Maryland. They specialized in catering to every variation of religious and ethnic mourning, burial, body preparation practice, and preference in the African diaspora. (This specialty was part of the reason Francine had chosen her field.) Every time she visited home, her father never failed to recount the story of how he and Francine's mother came from Montserrat to the States with nothing but $150 in his pocket and a one-month stay at a distant relative's home. When he's really amped up, he proudly describes how they were able to turn that little bit of money into a business that has been going strong for 25 years. Yes, hers was a proud family. One of the more prominent, black families in the

Silver Springs, MD, area. So food stamps could not to be in her future.

"Food stamps?!" shrieked the woman on the phone. "Wow. That's deep."

The woman was Francine's friend, Comfort. They'd grown up together and even attended the same college. They'd developed a strong friendship partially because of their Caribbean heritage—Comfort was Jamaican.

"Well, we know Papa Carty surely wouldn't stand for that!" Comfort continued.

"I knoooow. I wouldn't hear the end of it."

"Well …" Comfort paused, unsure of how to ask her friend the question. Francine could hear Comfort's two children playfully giggling in the background. "… do you need food?"

Switching her cell phone to the opposite ear, Francine used her free hand to open the refrigerator in her small galley kitchen. She rolled her eyes at the half-gallon of milk, plastic wrapped covered bowl of soup, and sleeve of saltine crackers.

"No. I'm alright," she says. "I'll make it."

"Sure, you will. I'll slip a little something in the mail to you this afternoon!"

Comfort spoke empathetically into the phone, turning up her accent for effect. "You are already a size 6 and beautiful. I don't need you eclipsing me entirely, ya hear?!"

Francine thanked her and zoned out.

***

A *Red Flyer* wagon. The bottom filled with large grey and brown and black rocks. Pulled roughly along the sidewalk by a wobbly, almond girl of 8 with thick, twisted ponytails and pink, Bubble-Yum tinted lips. She was purposeful. She had some place to be. The creek was her destination. To deliver the rocks. To do her part in the building of the fort. The fort that would house the secrets of little Frankie, her sister Robbi, and her friends. The place they'd come to dish about the Christmas gifts they found hidden in their parents' garages. Where they would come to cry when moms and dads yelled and drank and hit. It would be their safe place until the creek overflowed and washed it—and their secrets—away.

***

"Frankie! Paging, Dr. Frankie!" Comfort yelled. "You zoning out on me again?!"

It was a habit of Francine's. One she'd begun as a child and wasn't fully willing to break.

"I'm sorry, Sis. You know how I get lost in my thoughts."

"Uhh huh. Well anyway, I think I might be able to help you."

"Help me what?"

"Help you get some extra money—and not lose your pride in the process."

This time, Francine tuned in to her friend. Maybe this would be exactly what she needed.

***

"Phone sex operator?!" Francine said aloud to herself as she scrolled through the online application that Comfort had sent via email.

> *Do you have a great voice? We are looking for fun, open-minded individuals who are interested in becoming phone actors/actresses in the adult entertainment industry. Set your own hours, work from home, and make $25/hour to start! Apply today!*

After hitting send, she wrestled with this new "opportunity." She went to bed thinking about what this would mean. It's not that she was a prude. Far from it, actually. Francine considered herself a free woman. Liberal, even. It was just the idea that this was so far from how she envisioned her life. Too far from the life she'd worked so hard to get. *But everyone has their own route to happiness*, she thought. Maybe this was hers?

It was a fitful night, for sure. Francine awakened multiple times, roused by the recurring dream that had plagued her for weeks. She was standing in front of class, teaching, and as naked as a newborn. When she lifted her hands to gesture, she found that her hands were chained to the desk. That's when she noticed that her students weren't her students at all. They were children. All under 4 years old. Staring back at her, wide-eyed and attentive.

She had no idea what to make of it.

Four days later, she got the call.

"Ms. Carty?"

"This is Ms. Carty."

A brief pause then, "Aha. Your voice will work perfectly!"

Francine was hired for the night shift but was given the flexibility to change her schedule if she needed to do so. Everyone started on the night shift, the woman had said. It was "easier."

"We'll send someone out to you this afternoon to get you all set up. Will 2 p.m. work?"

"Set up?" Francine asked.

"Yes, we need to give you your 'work' phone, get your identification and HR paperwork completed, and …" The woman paused more for effect than hesitation. "… and train you."

Francine wasn't sure why she couldn't go their offices, why they needed to come to her home, but she didn't bother to question it. She simply scheduled the meeting for 2 until the woman's last words registered.

"Train?"

"Yes. There are some things you should be aware of. Questions you don't have to answer, things you don't have to do … you know, that kind of thing."

No, I don't know, Francine thought.

"We just like to cover all our bases. To make sure you're protected as well as our clients. Now … as far as payment …"

Now this is what Francine wanted to hear more about.

"It's $25 an hour just like the ad says. How would you like to be paid? Via check or electronically?"

Francine certainly didn't want there to be any evidence of her new job showing up in her bank account so she gave the woman the email address that was linked to her online payment application.

"The payments are weekly—every Friday—and will come from NTS Corporation. That way you're protected."

"Ah, okay. Thanks."

"So you're all set. Welcome aboard! Do you have any questions?" the woman's words blended together as she seemed to be rushing the overwhelmed Francine off of the phone.

"Uh, um, no. Not right now."

"Okay. Have fun!"

Fun.

I WISH I was doing this for fun.

***

Later that day, the technician/trainer, a stout woman with long locks who was ravishing a piece of gum, came to Francine's home with a large messenger backpack filled with papers, phones, and headsets.

"You have any toys?"

Francine was startled and didn't respond.

"No, no, no. I'm just asking because it's easier when you can get off too," the woman said nonchalantly.

"I guess," Francine responded.

"Okay, you're all set. Here's your headset. You'll probably need your hands free." The woman laughed at herself. "Calls usually start to come in promptly at 11. I hope you're not a heavy sleeper. You'll want to answer every call because they are definitely tracking you. When the phone rings, it will be the center. We'll brief you on the caller's preferences and the scenario, give you a chance to clear your voice—keep some water by the phone, then you're on with the caller. The script is just a guide, be creative. They can tell when your reading. The second they hear pages turning, they hang up—*scriptus interruptus*. Some nights you'll get four or five calls, some nights one or two. Sometimes none. Shut it down at four."

Francine wrote down the information on the white board she'd mounted in her kitchen.

"How many days per week are you working?"

"Three. For now."

The woman lifted the heavy bag onto her shoulder. "Okay, yeah. That's good. A cool 300 to 400 a week to do what you do for your man for free, right?"

The woman chuckled again and reminded Francine of the island Santa Clauses she'd see as a child when her family visited for the holidays.

The implications of what the woman said unsettled Francine so much that she rushed the woman out of her place.

"Okay, well, I have an appointment so I'd better start getting ready. Thanks for everything," she said.

The woman left, and Francine exhaled for what seemed like the first time that morning.

By the time 11 o'clock rolled around, Francine had stopped breathing again. She was terrified. She'd been told that she needed to come up with a name for herself, and she'd decided on Zora. At the time she'd come up with it, she thought it was clever. Now she wasn't so sure.

At 11:02, her "work" phone rang. The preboarding details were a blur. Then, "Showtime, Fran. Good luck!" It seemed like the person on the other end had gotten started without her.

"Just suck it, okay! Suck it hard now!"

Francine/Zora was so taken aback that she hit end on the phone before saying anything.

What am I doing?

The next call came in at 11:07. They gave her a pass on the maiden call, but warned if she couldn't cut it on the next one, her $25 first and final check would be in the mail.

"Hello?" she said, reaching for the deepest, sexiest, register she could.

"SINNER!"

Francine went quiet.

"Hello? Hello?" The raspy voice on the other end pled.

"Umm … y-y-yes. I'm here."

"REPENT! Your soul is damned to HELL!"

Francine hung up on the call quickly. Wrapping her arms around herself, she tried her best to detach. *You can do this!*

The dispatcher called. "We'll give you a pass on that one. Sometimes the zealots get through our screen. Our mistake. You sure you're up for this?"

Francine lied, and the third call came in at 11:22.

"Hello?"

She braced herself for violence but was met with the soft, rumble of a voice that seemed equally as nervous as her own.

"Hello."

Francine looked down at the script she'd been given.

"So, what's your pleasure, baby?"

There was a brief pause.

"Well … what are you wearing?"

How cliché, she thought.

Feeling bolder, she responded. "What do you want me to be wearing?"

"I want you to be my teacher," the voice said quietly.

Oh, the whole teacher-student fantasy. At least this was one role-play she'd actually done before.

"Okay, baby. So, what should I call you?"

Another pause.

"My name is Chase."

Francine laid back onto the full-sized bed in her small, studio apartment.

"Alright, Chase. What can Ms. Zora teach you tonight?"

2

Garrison's waiting was always part presentation, part contemplation. Francine liked to watch him. He had such ritualistic behaviors. The way he sat slightly slouched, one leg extended. The opposite arm resting on a table, his fingertips courting a drink he swirled by the rim as it swished around before taking just the tiniest sip. As she revealed herself, he looked over her intently. She was devastatingly average, he thought. Nothing about her in passing stood out. But a careful look revealed the most enchanting smile. With it, she had bewitched him in their very first encounter. It was her strategic advantage, and she wielded it masterfully. This both intrigued and frustrated him. She was so savvy socially but was spinning her wheels when it came to getting her professional life on track. And to be clear, anyone expecting a future with Garrison had better have herself together.

The first time Garrison saw Francine, she was unloading a mini-moving van in cut-off denim Daisy Duke shorts from which stemmed long, lean, strong, soft brown legs, a white razor-back brushed cotton t-shirt cradling perfect bouncy C cups. And to top it all off, she wore red high-top Chuck Taylor Converse sneakers that were just a little dirty. It was as if she was giving a show only for him as she bent, reached, and stretched to unload the mini-mover.

And she was.

Francine looked deep into her reluctant admirer's eyes for one full second and said, "Hey," with a smile that gleamed. Then she turned her head releasing the gaze just slow enough to let him see the smirk acknowledging his inability to do a damn thing in response.

The woman with him was clearly his girlfriend but was not at all paying attention. She had these eerie, dead eyes; windows to an empty soul, it seemed to Francine. Nevertheless, she could tell that Garrison was the kind of man who wouldn't dare disrespect his mate by engaging another woman publicly in anymore than a causal greeting. *No worries*, Francine thought. She was new in town and wanted no trouble. Francine sensed he was also the kind of man who would make his way to her when he was able.

One month, tops.

She could feel his determination. His aura had issued a challenge.

When he showed up in her early-morning *Black Life in Film and Literature* seminar the next week, a hot flash of panic waved through her body. *Please, God, don't tell me this man is one of my students!* She concluded the introductory lecture and began facilitating a discussion on the assigned reading, an essay about transgenerational trauma that she wanted students to think about as they began August Wilson's *Joe Turner's Come and Gone*.

After the class, Garrison lingered until everyone else left the room. He wore a luxurious apricot linen button-down shirt, the sleeves haphazardly rolled to the forearms. His fingers rested in the front pockets of a pair of expensive-looking jeans. His shoes, the color of cognac with hand-stitched soles, looked even more expensive. Francine's instant and intentional body scan read: 6'2", former college football player, not especially handsome but sexy as hell.

Damn. Stay cool. Professor mode, quick! she implored herself, wishing her face had not already registered recognition. iPad in hand, she had to spin it. She was, of course, the consummate professional.

"I believe you arrived a bit late. Let me adjust the attendance, Mr.?"

Garrison took the iPad from her and flung it onto the pile of books on the desk, returning the full second gaze she thought only she had mastered.

Aw, shucks, she thought, her temperature rising. Now, he was standing so close she could smell his scent and feel his body's warmth.

"I am Garrison McQueen. You know damned well I'm not enrolled in your class," his baritone voice penetrated her. Extending his hand, palm up, the remaining distance between them, he grasped hers and gave it a gentle but strong tug toward him. He paused, looking down at her, now brow to brow with her 5'5" frame.

"Dirty red," he said with a smirk.

After what seemed like forever, she spoke.

"Dirty red?" was all she could muster. But she was indignant.

"Yes. You were unforgettably cute in those dirty red Chucks you were wearing the other day." They both burst into laughter, breaking their little scene wide open.

"Oh, *that's* what you couldn't forget!?" she taunted in return.

"Well, your lecture was pretty good, too," he stepped back and they lapsed into more suitable introductory pleasantries.

***

Three years later, and they still enjoyed frequent rounds of cat and mouse. But most of the time, she watched him. Garrison was a contemplative man, while Francine was impulsive. It was the reason neither of them could fully commit to the relationship.

They were never really off. They just weren't always on.

Garrison was so intense with Francine. She didn't trust it. Not because she thought he was disingenuous, just the opposite. The relationship was just so full and complete and so … instantaneous. He cooked for her, introduced her to all of his friends, showed her around town, rubbed her feet, protected her, and kissed her passionately always. The conversations never ended, and their lovemaking always left them spent. It often began in exchanges like that of their first meeting. But mostly it was an all-day encounter:

caring morning check-ins, nice gestures, compliments, conversations, and laughter. By the end of the day, he was at her door, hungry from the day's hunt. Her defenses were gone. The evening's dance ensued: a bite to eat, a sip of wine, a caress, an embrace. By the time they reached her bedroom, all inhibitions were gone. They made love unselfishly and completely. After, they slept in each other's arms until morning. In the early days, he would ask her what she liked and how she liked it. Francine gave no instructions, only motivation.

"Hold my wrists," she heaved under his body weight, everything throbbing well into their first half hour of bliss.

"You have cuffs?" he asked in a gruff throaty voice, surprised.

She looked into his eyes and played his ego, "Cuffs? Don't you know what you're doing?"

It was on. Garrison intertwined her fingers with his and raised them above her head outstretched. He released them and grasped her wrists firmly. Her eyes locked with his letting him know she relinquished her body to his. He watched her as their rhythm synced and they became one. Her face told their story: Her eyes closed as they moved in harmony, her furrowed brow marked her resistance to the pleasure she felt. She turned away, involuntarily contorted her expression—precursor to the release that would soon follow.

"Look at me, Francine" Garrison quietly commanded.

Francine obeyed, her open eyes revealing utter and complete surrender. Garrison smiled in triumph, released her wrists and held her by the waist, his hands almost encircling it. Slowly, he rubbed his large hands up the sides of her buttery-smooth torso, then wrapped his arms around her in a tight embrace supporting her now wobbly head with one hand, tears rolling back toward her ears. He joined her surrender. And so it went between them.

***

But Garrison was selfish and hurt. Francine was his cake. When they met, he had a girlfriend of several years. Her family was wealthy and prominent, and he never felt he matched up. He desperately wanted the brass ring of a trophy wife, but it was Francine who made him laugh, kept him honest, and matched his wit. Francine indeed loved Garrison, as a friend and as a lover. But because things began so abruptly with him and he was so naked with his emotions, she needed to peer at him under the glass jar at times. Francine was never sure if he was seeking in her what he could not attain with the princess trophy.

On one day in particular, she watched carefully. She tried to read his mood. What would be on their lunch menu today: a lecture, adoration, humor, campus gossip, an argument perhaps? Would they talk as best friends or lovers? Francine could never tell. But she liked trying.

Garrison liked putting on the show. Francine was pretty transparent in the way she examined him. Sometimes she inventoried his physique, other times his demeanor. He knew his confidence—or maybe it was arrogance—was as attractive to Francine as her feigned oblivion of her own sex appeal was to him. He knew she needed her mate to appreciate her primarily for her mind and personality, so she downplayed her femininity. Most of the time, she dressed younger than her age or wore her clothes a size too big. She also pretended to ignore or not understand sexual innuendo from strangers and older male colleagues. In truth, it was a defense mechanism to protect her from predators. She moved a lot and lived alone.

But Garrison recognized her mask immediately and penetrated it like a laser. From the very moment he saw her, Garrison knew Francine needed him and he wanted to take care of her. They never spoke the words, it just was. It was how they related to each other. The intimacy they shared on absolutely every level was intense. Strangers sensed it. Friends and family could see it. Francine and Garrison were the only holdouts.

***

Francine hated to admit it, but she became overly self-conscious when she knew she was meeting Garrison. She always felt like he was appraising her. Not in a pimp or slave girl for sale manner. Still, something that felt unintentionally similar. So, she brushed the short, soft edges of her hair one too many times. Then ran her fingers through it in defiance. The reflection in her mirror was shaking her head and chastising for her ridiculous obsession. In a huff, she'd walked to the full-length mirror in her closet to make sure her dress was right. She had chosen an innocent-looking sundress. It was off-white with nickel-sized pale yellow and peach flowers. The straps crossed in the back requiring a strapless bra.

"Shoot!" she exclaimed. She'd forgotten to put on lotion before her skin dried. She ran back to the bathroom to dampen her arms and legs, then applied the honeysuckle-scented body lotion she concocted herself with a mixture of hypoallergenic fragrance-free lotion and essential oil. Francine liked her legs to glow. It took her forever to treat the eczema that plagued her for years. Now that she had found the right moisturizers and stopped taking hell-hot showers, her skin rewarded her with touchable softness that she cared for meticulously.

Francine finally felt cute enough but needed a pop of wow. She rifled through her rarely used cosmetic bag for the lipsticks she bought with the last gift card from Christmas to help her get into character for her new gig: *Ready Red* and *Ablaze*. *Ablaze*, the daring orange with a satin finish, would provide the perfect contradiction to the girl-next-door sundress. Perfection! If Garrison responded to it, maybe it would boost her confidence with her callers. The French pedicure Garrison treated her to a few days ago was still unchipped, so she burrowed into the pile of shoes on the floor of her closet for the strappy wedge peep-toe sandals which accented the anklet she wore throughout the summer months.

"It's in the details, baby girl," she said blowing a kiss at her reflection. Francine grabbed her keys and headed out the door.

She parked the rattling hunk of metal that she, on the one hand, resented as a symbol of her being perpetually on the verge of something great—but never actually getting "there." On the other hand, she praised for ride for a job well done every time it got her to point B. This day, though, the rattling betrayed her pre-event voyeurism. Besides, Garrison was likely in the middle of a lab test of some sort with limited time. Still, she didn't hurry. Instead, she got out of the car and walked toward him smiling inwardly at his gentleman of leisure entitlement. He sat, a fixture of sorts, warmed by the sun, yet shaded from its glare, even caressed by the breeze. He looked so self-assured, seemingly taking up all the space under the patio table, its large canvas umbrella and more. Dining alfresco suited him.

"Is that brown liquor in your glass in the middle of the day?" Francine smiled that smile of hers.

"You know you're my only drug of choice," he said, gesturing for her to take a seat. "You look good."

Garrison admired the effortlessness of her casual beauty. After wearing every variation of relaxer, braids, and kinky twists, her recent hairstyle, a short, cropped natural, made him want to touch her—all the time. The cut drew attention to her large brown eyes and the lips that harbored the kryptonite smile and promised the sweetest, most delicious kisses. One taste and his heart, wallet, and zipper were open for the taking. She knew it. Hell, everyone knew it and he didn't care.

"Why thank you, kind gentleman," she turned on a 19th century, southern accent.

Garrison chuckled. "You're crazy. Come over here next to me, Frankie. I ordered salmon Caesars. I need to get back to the lab soon. Are you done for the day?"

"So demanding," Francine replied, bending to kiss him on the cheek.

"I'm good right here on this side of the table," she said, removing his hand from the back of her thigh. It had deftly found its way under her knee-length sundress.

"A salad is just what I had in mind, thank you. And, yes, I am done with class for the day."

Garrison stared at her with the excruciating intensity that had her running around her apartment earlier trying to look her absolute best.

"That lipstick is crazy, but it looks good on you," he said. "Maybe I need to be finished in the lab for the day. My imagination is taking those lips someplace."

"You are so nasty!" Francine said as she thanked the server who brought their salads and inwardly congratulated herself on her choice of lip color weaponry.

"Nice and nasty," he said, imitating the satisfied commendation he often earned from her.

"Well, I do like you nasty," she confessed, indulgently. "You make me sick."

"For real, what's up with that color?" he asked.

"You are such a girl, G. I'm just trying a new color," she said off-handedly.

"You need some groceries, baby? You're killing that salad?" Garrison asked half-jokingly.

"I *am* killing it! I didn't realize how hungry I was," she said before stuffing another heaping forkful into her orange-ish lips.

She dabbed the corners of her mouth and giving her best "Prissy Prudy" imitation.

"Actually, yes. I could use a few dollars for groceries until I get paid Friday. You are looking at a new consultant with NTS Company!" she announced hoping against hope he wouldn't ask for details.

"NTS? Wait a minute. Girl, you're a phone sex operator?!" he said in a cocktail of awe, shock, and judgment.

"HOW THE HELL DO YOU KNOW NTS?!" Francine shouted, laughing in disbelief.

"Oh my God—one of my housemates back in undergrad used to call them. We had this fat-ass phone bill one month and none of us knew who NTS was. When we finally called the number, he 'fessed up. He owed like $250! We called his ass NTS for a year! I almost forgot all about that!"

They laughed long and hard and spent the rest of the lunch rehashing her foibles during the first night of calls. Their conversation then turned to thinking up "call" girl names, finally resting on "the naughty professor." They knew that ultimately they would use it only for themselves, along with dirty red, but it was fun to brainstorm with him. Plus, Francine was already committed to *Zora*.

After the laughs were exhausted, Garrison turned to Francine. "Frankie baby, you're better than that shit. You're too smart. You need to find something else. Can't you talk to someone in your department about some research or something? I'll see what I can do, too."

"I know, but I have bills to pay *today*," she said soberly, wiping the tears of laughter mixed with self-pity.

"Liberal arts does *not* pay like engineering. Y'all have grant money for days! Trust me, I'm trying."

"I know you are. I got you for groceries. Just let me know if you need anything else, promise?" he said, standing up to hug her goodbye.

"Call me if you want a ride to the market. I can take you tomorrow."

Garrison did most of the basic maintenance on her car, but it needed a radiator that he couldn't quite afford at the moment so he'd often just drive her where she needed to go. He knew she appreciated his help, and he loved being her hero, even on his modest post-doc fellowship salary.

"I'll swing by your place later with the cash."

Francine leaned into his hug, "Thanks, G. You take such good care of me."

"Always, Girl," he said kissing the crown of her head. "I need to run. Later."

"Bye." Francine stood and watched Garrison trot to his midnight blue Honda Accord and peel off toward the campus. Francine was glad today was a *best friend* lunch.

***

The market bustled with after-work granola grains: people who worked for non-profits and universities and listened to National

Public Radio; the securely middle and upper classes; and those, like her, who were simply splurging on a rare but necessary trip to the all organic grocery. Francine fit into in the last category. She went straight for the dairy section for her high-end Greek yogurt and sent Garrison to taste the soups. Everything was so high there, but the quality was undeniable.

They did most of the shopping at the regular market. The stop at Whole Foods was just for a few items she would prepare for tonight's dinner. Whenever Garrison sprang for groceries, she prepared the first meal for him in appreciation. She had decided to make grilled chicken breast with a veggie medley of summer squash, and red and orange peppers sautéed with fresh baby spinach. She would serve it atop garlicky mashed potatoes with Old Bay steamed shrimp chopped in. A raspberry and lemon sorbet would suffice for dessert. Her last bottle of Riesling was chilling in the fridge. Garrison lost track of her in the store after his soup selection. He didn't understand how she enjoyed soup in the summer, but he obliged. He found her just along the back-aisle poultry section and watched her from the coffee station as she asked the butcher questions he couldn't determine from the distance. He could, however, determine that the 60ish man was more than happy to engage her inquiry. He watched as Francine turned on the charm, leaving the counter with twice as much chicken breast as she would pay for.

"Shameless!" he whispered in her ear as she approached him.

"What are you talking about!?" she laughed. "You always think I'm flirting with some man."

"You are, but I'm the one taking you home," he cupped the back of her neck, playfully.

She laughed, "That's right!"

They walked toward the check out. "So, how much extra chicken did he give you?" he asked.

"Oh, shut up," Francine giggled as she playfully hit Garrison with the 5-pound package of hormone-free, skinless, boneless chicken breast that the butcher had marked 3 pounds. He walked briskly ahead of her, "If your ass gets arrested at checkout, call Pop-Pop the butcher for the bail!"

Francine stood ahead of Garrison in the long line. He examined her: the delicate anklet that adorned her foot, the smooth slight curve of her calves that she flexed whenever she stood still for any length of time. The loose-fitting white sheath dress only hinted at what he knew was beneath: a recreational runner's taut, elastic thighs, slim hips, and a smooth stomach with a small black mole just left of her navel that winked at him whenever he looked at her naked body.

"Next!" the cashier's voice pulled him back.

The line moved up as the woman ahead of them unloaded the green handbasket onto the conveyor belt. Garrison's strong arms encircled Francine's slightly sculpted shoulders from behind. He rested his chin on top of her head. Francine relaxed into his broad chest.

Damn, I love this woman! He thought.

3

1994 – Hampton, VA

The house was dark. Not pitch-black, can't-see-in-front-of-your-face dark. More like the deep, shadowy gray of a house where it's obvious that no one is home. Francine jammed her keys into the lock and pushed open the door brusquely. She wobbled a bit as she balanced her book bag on one shoulder and three plastic grocery bags in the other hand. The door swung wide, the knob filling the dent that had formed months prior on the wall behind it.

"Of course she's not home," Francine said aloud to herself. She found it interesting that the very reasons why she wanted to move off campus were the same reasons she missed living there. But she loved having her own space—or somewhat her own space. Francine shared the rented corner house in the neighborhood adjacent to the school with a girl she'd met on the first day of her freshman year.

Kelly was local. She'd grown up in Norfolk and her whole family lived in the area. For Francine, it was cool to have a friend who knew every nook and cranny of the Hampton Roads—and had a car. Even better, Kelly was always down for a road trip to Maryland whenever Francine found herself missing home. Cherry blossoms, Boogie's Diner, Haines Point, and Pentagon City Mall were nothing but a few hours' ride up Route 13 in Kelly's baby blue Ford Topaz. Of course, Francine had other good friends—Comfort being one of them—but during Comfort's semester of study abroad, Francine and Kelly became tighter than tight.

It was their junior year—well, actually it was Francine's junior year, Kelly had changed majors twice already and was technically a sophomore—they decided to rent the little house on Breckinridge Street. They'd taken to calling themselves Hampton's Thelma and Louise for no other reason than that's the first movie they'd seen on their first double date. Kelly and Derek. Francine and Roderick. Roderick was long a memory for Frankie by the time she and Kelly moved into the house but she still looked forward to the fun times they'd have together. And, in the beginning, they certainly had a blast. From parties to study sessions to heated discussion on what South Africa should do next now that Apartheid had ended and Nelson Mandela was president, their house was the place to be. The only wrench in their good time was that it usually was never just Frankie and Kelly running things in the house. It was Frankie, Kelly, and Derek.

Kelly's boyfriend from back home was a regular fixture around the house and, at first, this was cool with Frankie. What's the point of having a house off campus if your boyfriend can't hang out there? But Derek's constant presence began to annoy Frankie after a while—especially since he stayed drunk and was an ugly, loud, violent drunk. Nevertheless, as long as he didn't bother her or do anything too crazy, she considered him a small price to pay for independence.

After placing her bag and the groceries down on the floor, Francine sifted through the mail basket that sat on a small, wooden table in the foyer. She separated the now bills from the later bills, picked back up the grocery bags, and headed to the kitchen. When she stepped across the threshold into their kitchen/living room combo, her stomach flipped and began churning as her eyes went wide with shock at the sight before her.

Kelly was sitting in one of the vinyl chairs that was part of the retro-'50s dining set they'd rescued during one of their notorious dumpster-diving expeditions. Her mouth was taped with the silver duct tape they used to fix everything from walls to extension cords. Her arms were bound together with the black wires of the jumper cables they kept in the small hallway that led to the basement.

Kelly's hair sat messily on her head like a bird's nest in progress, and her eyes, one blackened and bruised, were swollen with fear. Dark tracks of mascara lined her cheeks. She was wearing nothing but turquoise panties and the large, muscular arm of her boyfriend draped around her neck.

Derek's other hand held a small black and silver handgun with the barrel digging into the side of Kelly's tilted nest of a head.

"You have two choices, Frankie. Join her or turn around and walk away," he growled. "This has nothing to do with you."

Kelly's good eye pleaded for help as more tears planned their escape. Francine had no idea what to do. As a reflex, she scratched the back of her neck and was struck with how much sweat had accumulated there so quickly.

No sudden moves, she thought. She'd remembered that this was the mistake of most people on her favorite crime shows like *Twin Peaks* and *Law and Order*. But this wasn't a nighttime drama and no one was going to yell cut. She had to think fast.

Francine looked back at Kelly, then at Derek. He waved the gun toward her.

"Go on, Frankie, go on!"

She ducked out of the path of his reckless waving of the gun and fell against the wall. Her breath picked up its pace.

"Whatchugonnado, nah?" he slurred.

Should have known he was drunk.

Kelly's eyes closed. She seemed to be slipping in and out of consciousness. If her eyes were blackened, no telling what else was wrong, Francine considered. For a split second, she thought about her alleged options. If she left, her friend would likely be hurt. If she stayed, they'd both be in danger. Plus, who's to say he'd really let her leave. Knowing that she'd likely go call the police and get help, he'd probably just shoot her in the back. But that really wasn't the issue. Maybe it should've been but it wasn't. Kelly was her friend.

Despite her flighty ways and inability to keep the house clean, regardless of her poor choice in men and her apathy regarding school, Kelly was her girl and Francine took their relationship seriously. She loved her deeply and knew what she had to do.

Steeling herself against what she thought would surely be death by a barrage of bullets, Francine walked directly toward Derek. Kelly suddenly sat up and began bouncing in the chair, wiggling against the jumper cables that were tied around her arms as if Frankie's courage gave her renewed strength.

"Wait, wait, wait a minute, Frankie!" Derek flustered. Francine's boldness caught him off guard. He waved the gun wildly. This time, Francine did not duck, bob, or weave.

"This ain't got nothing to do with you, gul!"

Francine stopped in front of the two. Since she hadn't been shot, she decided to appeal to Derek's rational side. She wasn't sure, though, if he had one.

"D, you don't want to do this, man! You love Kelly. Why would you want to hurt her?" Francine made sure she kept her hands where he could see them.

Her words must have shaken him.

"Naw, naw, naw!" Derek yelled, his southern accent drawing and stretching each word. "She's got one more time to be smiling in that old dude's face. One more time!"

Francine looked at Kelly. *What old dude?* As if responding to Francine's telepathic signal, Kelly shook her head wildly and leaned her head in the direction of her books on the kitchen table.

"Her professor?!" Francine said as she turned just in time to see glints of metal slam down in the direction of her friend's head.

"Nooooooo!" she screamed and, in that moment, decided to risk it all.

Francine took three quick steps to the right and picked up from the coffee table a 1980s ceramic and brass lamp she'd taken from her parents' loaded garage six months earlier. She'd put it there that morning because she'd intended to buy a new lampshade at Ames the next day.

Divine providence leaned mercifully in her favor and changed her plans.

Derek, in his drunkenness, had missed Kelly's head. To recover, he reached out to grab Francine but also missed her, if only by an inch or so. He stumbled forward as the gun flew out of his hand and spun on its trigger across the old hardwood floors.

Francine, with all the strength she could muster and a healthy dose of adrenaline, brought the lamp down on Derek's head. Peach ceramic pieces rained down on them as he fell onto the floor, knocked out cold.

Francine ran over to Kelly and ripped the tape off her mouth. Her friend screamed.

"Oh no! I'm so, so, so, so, sorry, Frankie," Kelly mumbled over and over again as she looked back and forth between her friend and her man. Francine removed the cables and helped her friend to her feet. Kelly winced in pain. *Maybe her ribs were broken?*

Half dragging Kelly out the door, Frankie began yelling so the neighbors would hear her. She wasn't sure how long Derek would be out.

"Please call the police! Please help us!" she yelled.

A man in his late 40s with a salt-and-pepper goatee and a more conservative version of the box hairstyle opened his door and saw the two girls. He immediately told his wife to call the police and ran out to help. He carried Kelly into to his house and Francine followed.

When the police arrived minutes later, the officers shouted into a bullhorn, demanding that Derek give himself up. When Derek responded, Francine shook with fear. He was awake. Would there be a shoot out? She'd never been involved in anything like this in her life. After the 45-minute standoff, Derek exited the house with his hands in the air. Several officers tackled him to the ground, pulled his arms behind his back into handcuffs, and put him into the patrol car.

Inside their neighbors home, the police got more information from Kelly and Frankie before leaving the paramedics to examine them. Both of the EMTs said they were sure Kelly's ribs were not broken but still recommended that she be transported to the hospital. Francine was shocked when Kelly refused.

"What? Why not?!"

"I'm alright, Frankie. Don't worry. I don't need no hospital!" Kelly closed her eyes in defiance.

The paramedics packed their bags and equipment. One of them, a white guy with a short, blond buzz cut and emerald green eyes, shook his head as he walked out of the room. Francine tried to ignore what she'd clearly heard him mumble under his breath, "He'll kill her next time."

***

As far as Francine was concerned, there would never be a next time. *My girl is way too smart for that.* For the next three weeks, she nursed Kelly back to relative health. Relative because, well, she knew her friend was not just broken physically. She was severely heartbroken. Kelly had been with Derek since she was 14 years old. She'd endured much from him but as far as Francine knew, nothing to this extent. Being five years older than her, he wasn't just a boyfriend. He was a father figure. He'd protected her from the rages of her mother and the religion of her grandmother. He was the one who said she'd be better suited to be a teacher even though she'd entered college with dreams of being a television reporter. She believed him and changed her major.

To Francine, he'd always been controlling, even verbally abusive. But she'd never judged her friend for being with him prior to the incident at the house. He was Kelly's weakness. Francine had her own.

But after the incident at their house, everything was different. Kelly had pressed charges, and Derek was in jail. Everything would be okay, Francine thought. Eventually.

A month later, Francine awakened to strange noises outside her bedroom.

"Kels?" she called out.

No answer.

She could hear the noise—it sounded like someone breathing—getting louder and louder. The voice was deep, raspy even, and this caused Francine to tremble. Since the episode with Derek, she'd taken to sleeping with a large, butcher knife in the drawer of her nightstand. Not wanting to take any chances, she grabbed the knife and opened the door to her room.

Glimmers of the rising morning sun sliced the darkness in the hallway. She followed the sound of the breathing feeling strangely like the main character in a horror flick. A slow moan accompanied the breathing along with a knocking noise. The knife shook in Francine's hands. As she turned the corner into the living room, she was stunned.

Kelly was on her knees, bobbing her head between two long, muscular, Hershey legs. Her friend didn't see Francine, but Derek did. With a sly smirk on his face, he winked at Francine.

Her heart beat wildly in her chest as she ran back into her room, shut and locked the door, and began packing her bag. She'd risked her life for her friend, someone that she'd allowed to get close to her, and this was how she was repaid.

Francine knew all the statistics about abused women. About how many of them take back their abusers. And in another life, she might have been able to muster up some sister-girl compassion for her friend. But Francine had relinquished the last of her empathy a month prior when she'd faced Derek's gun. There was nothing left to give.

That early morning in 1994 had changed her. Kelly and Derek had become the default cautionary tale that motivated Francine. When she considered dropping out of her PhD program, she would persevere as if not completing it would somehow cast her under the influence of some ne'er-do-well like Derek. She would share her experience with her female friends and students as a reality check for what can happen in unhealthy relationships. It was why she always lived alone. It was why no man she dated *ever* got a set of her keys. No matter the void that was filled by a suitor, a singular misstep could set him back to day one. That spring of 1994 was her iron curtain. So when she took the NTS calls, she would convince herself that fiber optic distance allowed *her* to be in control of the weirdoes, crazies, pervs, and the strikingly normal people who paid her to talk to them.

It was a work call that awakened her that night bringing back the spring of 1994. The caller said his name was Derek and he wanted her to polish his gun. Off script, "Zora" aggressively suggested that she pistol-whip him instead. Just as she tried to recover her character, the caller began whimpering in a high-pitched, voice, "Don't whip me. I'll be a good boy. DD is a good boy, Mommeeeee!" What the ... ?? Forty-five minutes later, Zora had finally wrapped up with *DD* after listening to the caller's confessions about oral fixations that began with thumb sucking and escalated to all kinds of appendages. She was amazed at how she refrained from bursting into laughter. Then again, she knew precisely how—the bonus money for keeping a caller on the line longer than 20 minutes was a powerful restraint. She had doubled a full night's wages in that one call! Thirty minutes into the call, Zora had removed *Ready Red* lipstick, replacing it with the vitamin E she obsessively applied to her lips overnight. She could roll over and go to sleep now. Francine wondered if Kelly's Derek had some kind of fixation. She prayed Kelly had found her way clear of him.

Just as her shift was ending, a second call came in, rousing her from a good REM sleep. Francine reached for the *Ready Red* lipstick to get into character, then placed it back on her nightstand—an upside down cardboard box covered with a beautiful square yard of red, purple, green, and gold silk fabric she bought in China a few summers ago—another artifact of the paradox that was her life. It was her regular, Chase. Chase began requesting Zora two to three nights a week. He was pretty consistent. He mostly wanted her to describe what she was wearing and for Zora to talk about holding *him in her* arms, spooning. Easy money, Francine thought. She didn't even need her lipstick for this. Vitamin E would do for him.

Over the weeks, the calls from Chase grew longer and longer. They were up to 20 minutes, but Chase was careful never to carry the conversation into the bonus pricing. By now, Chase did most of the talking. He talked about intimate longings he felt he could never have. Chase just seemed lonely and wanted someone to talk to and listen. Francine offered Zora's best listening ear. Chase was witty, charming, and seemed at the top of his game, professionally. But his personal life lacked any kind of dimension. It was sad. She could tell he didn't trust her but wanted to. It was as if she were a full hall closet. He would open the door, whisper his secrets into the darkness, then slam the door shut as if they might spill out otherwise.

Several conversations later, Chase revealed he had been married long ago but wouldn't talk about why it ended. He began asking more questions about Zora, her day job—treading dangerously close to the "confidentiality protection" clause in her work agreement. Francine began looking forward to Chase's calls. He brought normalcy to the gig. Theirs became kind of a friendship with walls.

They both understood the boundaries and pushed but did not cross. Instead, they ventured into other interesting areas. Chase was well traveled, spoke hospitality levels of several languages, and was fluent in Spanish and Portuguese. He shared escapades about lovers he'd met around the world, while Zora listened. Chase didn't seem at all interested in exploring fantasies with Zora. He just needed to verbalize his own. As long as Chase was on the clock, Zora was all ears.

***

Francine's morning lecture seemed to get earlier and earlier. Or so it felt. The late-night listening was catching up to her. This morning, she compensated by having students spend the first 15 minutes of class viewing a filmed scene of *the play* they were reading that did not have dialogue, then asking the students to try to write the scene's stage directions, all while she finished her coffee, took attendance, and planned the next 60 minutes of class. Finally, she was awake enough to teach.

"In teams of three, work together to rewrite the direction. The rewrite should reflect the best of each group member's individual work."

Francine instructed them to use the large Post-it flip pages stored in the back of the room to write and post their final drafts. Circulating around the room, she listened to the groups go over each other's directions, arguing over what was supposed to be explicit or implicit. She called time, and each team had to post their directions on any free wall space around the room. They spent the final 30 minutes critiquing each team's work as a class and at the end reading the screenwriter's directions to see how theirs compared.

By 9:15, the elixir of caffeine and successfully engaged students had worked its magic. Francine was wide-awake.

"Great work, everyone. You rocked this exercise! I can't wait to read your papers!" she pushed their pride and panic buttons at once.

"Ugghh, why'd you have to spoil a good class, Professor?" sulked a young lady quickly becoming Francine's favorite student for her unfiltered self-expression.

"Oh, Renee. You've had something insightful to say about all of the material we've covered on this play. I'm sure your paper will be a masterpiece of revelation," Francine encouraged her and the other students as they exited the room into the now bustling hallway.

Before gathering her things to clear out for the next instructor, Francine quickly edited and saved the exercise she had pulled together. She'd tweak it a bit more and file it in the Exercises folder for the class.

"I love this class," she said to herself as she stuffed her tattered August Wilson compilation, notes, and laptop into her bag to walk down the hall where she would teach her 9:30 class.

In the new classroom, Francine adjusted the lights for the viewing and completed the login to use the smart technology built into the podium. She ran back to the last class to retrieve her coffee cup before it was discarded as trash and decided that a refill was in order. Her belongings secure—a few students had arrived early to class—she greeted them and walked down the hall to the departmental office to fill up.

"Good morning, Francine. I just put on a fresh pot," Noah greeted her. He was quite the rarity: a male administrative assistant.

"Good morning, Noah. Thanks for the 8 o'clock pot! It saved me this morning," Francine said. "You deserve a medal."

"I'll take that, thank you. Now that we have to get Jasper on the school bus at the crack of dawn, I can get here a little early to get some things done before the day gets crazy—including coffee for the early starters" Noah said.

Raising her cup, "Cheers to you *and* Jasper, then. I'm sure we all appreciate your thoughtfulness," Francine said. She added cream and sugar to her second cup.

Francine did appreciate him. Noah was very good at his job, and most of the faculty generously told him so. Then, there were the others who operated on a caste system in which administrative assistants—and adjunct professors like her—were almost invisible and treated as dispensable distractions with nuisance concerns. Well, maybe just the adjuncts. The administrative assistants, who usually buried the proverbial bones, were sometimes treated delicately. Still, they were often unduly regarded as an underclass.

Francine took a sip as she exited the office toward her class. "Delish," she sighed indulgently.

"You look like you're having a good morning or better yet, had a good night?" said a familiar voice, mocking Francine's liquid escape.

Francine looked up from her coffee.

"Oh, Roseline, hello. You've interrupted my morning worship!"

Francine laughed as she greeted the university's first female endowed chair and the dean of the College of Arts and Sciences, Dr. Roseline Mercer. Dr. Mercer was both respected and a little feared by the faculty, Francine included. Her reputation was well founded. Then assistant professor, Roseline Mercer was rumored to have been responsible for taking down the president at her previous institution for underwriting a culture of gender discrimination that involved research funding, salary, teaching load, and tenure discrepancies. Apparently, Roseline found herself in the eye of the storm, unintentionally, but fought hard and smart—calling on senior contacts from the Women in Higher Ed United for Progress (WHUP)—to emerge from the mess intact, and with a mammoth settlement to boot. *WHUP* him they did! She was quietly recruited to Ravencrest the following summer. Her arrival touched off the university's equity initiative that resulted in a far better workplace for faculty and staff of protected classes. The chair's demeanor was pleasant and understated, unless a situation called for her inner warrior.

"That must be some coffee. I'll have to make sure Noah keeps it in stock. Good day," she smiled and kept walking, never missing a step.

Like everyone else, Francine respected and admired Roseline, but unlike them, the fear had fallen away. The deep lines in her face initially seemed to represent the epic battle scars from the trenches. But now, after several conversations over the semesters, Roseline transformed from superhuman to a super person many faculty aspired to emulate in some fashion. The deep lines inscribed in her brow and around her mouth probably came from any number of life's stresses. Her Peruvian ancestry tinted her skin, but she was a Texan through and through. When called for, she talked tough and delivered. Her office was an eclectic mix of Southwestern, Peruvian, and touches of African and Caribbean furnishings, crafts, artwork, and literature.

One could never predict what kind of music might be wafting from Roseline's office to intrigue or delight passersby. Her wardrobe was even more unpredictable—prairie boots and denim one day, tailor-made designer pinstripes with power shirt and pumps the next. She was interesting and frankly, could wear anything. She was tall, lean, and an avid cyclist. Her dark hair seemed a bit disheveled on one side most of the time, likely due to some nervous habit, Francine hadn't figured out yet. But anyone could tell it was salon maintained. Roseline always appeared well put together. Francine had attended a few of her "celebrity scholar-advocate" talks. The audience, Francine included, were duly rapt. Roseline's voice, a raspy tenor—much like Francine imagined hers would become in 30 years, was easy listening. Roseline's way with words, juxtaposing unassuming anecdotes with sledgehammer consequences, statistics, or conclusions was why she was paid the big bucks. Without being a show-person, Roseline wowed the audience every time. But Francine mostly found her intriguing for what she didn't say. Roseline, for all the publications, interviews, speaking engagements, and advocacy was just a bit uncomfortable in her skin. Oddly, Francine felt a kinship and decided to like her.

***

Francine stood in the foyer of The Hibiscus Suite faculty dining hall feeling, for lack of better descriptor, *between*. She belonged, but not fully; she was an *associate* member of sorts. It was the same feeling she had in Whole Foods. She shared the values of the organic, crunchy, granola NPR colony, but neither made the income nor carried the rank to fully express those values. Likewise, at the faculty dining hall, she had earned the PhD, read all the right books, lived in the right neighborhood, and even had the same high-tech accessories (thanks to Garrison's technology jones). But she was the one who stretched her budget $25 to splurge on a few favorite items at Whole Foods. Since her faculty appointment was only part-time, she earned a fraction of the salaries her similarly credentialed colleagues earned. In addition to not being able to afford meals at the dining hall daily, she felt as if she were an awkward hybrid: part entitled, part interloper.

"Hey, Girlfriend. Sorry, I'm late," Ursula panted, catching her breath. The speed walk from her office and up the two flights of stairs to the dining room served as one of her many mini-cardio surges of the day.

"Whew!" Ursula exhaled. "That was for dessert!"

Francine smiled at her friend and reminisced about their first meeting.

***

Ursula was one of Francine's absolutely favorite people at Ravencrest. She was 100% all of the time. No pretense, no apology, no puffery. Ursula and Francine met during new faculty orientation. Although Ursula was full-time and on a tenure track, she sat in on the adjunct orientation because it included breakfast.

"Until I get paid and reimbursed for relocation, I will partake of every free meal I can find on this campus. They always feed the adjuncts well, because they pay slave wages. It's the least they could do. You know you're hungry!" she nudged Francine's elbow.

Francine wanted to be insulted but couldn't help herself. Instead, she smiled in relief that someone knew her pain. Ursula proceeded to participate attentively. Three hours later, she convinced Francine to join her for lunch at the orientation for new full-time faculty. Reluctantly, she consented. Francine, having come from a family of some means had long since learned how to posture just enough to fit into an environment that was a smidge above her own class. But it still always made her uncomfortable.

"Professor Ursula St. James," she confidently announced herself as if attending a State dinner. The attendant presented her with a nametag that read, *Ursula St. James, PhD.*

"Crap!" Francine thought. Before she could panic at the thought of being turned away, mortified, Ursula continued. "Thank you. My colleague Dr. Francine …?"

"Carty" Francine chimed in making eye contact and smiling at the blondish woman in her 30s who greeted them.

"Yes, Dr. Francine Carty's nametag seems to be missing. This is the second time today. Is this going to be a problem for the orientation?" Ursula asked warmly.

"Dr. Carty, of course. I do recall the name. We've a few nametags and markers in case we missed someone. Please, forgive the oversight. It's hectic this time of year but shouldn't be a problem going forward. Welcome! I'm Beverly. I'm the person taking care of things to get you settled—campus ID, parking decals, office keys, etc."

"Thank you very much, Beverly," Francine and Ursula said practically in unison, their conspiracy successful.

One behind the other, they filed along the lunch buffet piling their plates with salad, sandwich halves, pickles, chips, and cookies. They found seats in the middle of the high-tech smart classroom, clearly showing off the campus' latest capital improvements.

"*St. James*?!" Francine queried Ursula, in a whisper as if sharing a secret with a childhood friend.

Francine was so preoccupied with her *actual* orientation, she hadn't paid much attention to the scratchy blue letters Ursula had written on the white adhesive square stuck to her blouse before discarding it ceremoniously as they exited the old classroom where the breakfast orientation was held. She was sure it simply read *Ursula.* Or did it? Francine really didn't remember. In any case, she now knew that Ursula was a *St. James*.

"Yep," Ursula said, looking at Francine with sad eyes trying to determine how the name would matter.

Ursula St. James was the daughter of famous-turned-infamous parents—at least among the black elite who had the influence to keep the scandal out of the media. Francine, despite her current situation as a pauper, had enjoyed loose social ties with the upper-class families in the Caribbean and Virginia because of her family's business. And the St. Jameses were the uppermost upper crust. The family had long held prominence in Haiti and America mostly due to undocumented connections to the black aristocracy emergent after the Haitian Revolution, as well as subsequent free communities in the American South.

The Jameses were part of the less well-known but intricate network of maritime Underground Railroad conductors. In addition to countless grateful African Americans, among their clients were wealthy white Americans and Europeans who made handsome but confidential off-shore payments of prime property in order to safely transport mistresses, family miscreants, and of course, tinted offspring to other parts of the world. Brothers, Captains Jean and Robert St. James were visionaries. For generations, they were heralded as revolutionary royalty.

A few years ago, the name was sullied by a salacious property dispute involving the great-great-grandsons of the brothers. Cousins, Bernard and Yves St. James, Ursula's father and cousin, respectively, were both named in her mother's will as equal beneficiaries of her family estate in Virginia. Ursula's mother, Penelope Lafayette St. James, apparently had an affair with her husband's perpetual bachelor cousin, Yves, claiming her husband knew but didn't care. As real estate was her husband's only true love, this was her parting "gift." Knowing better, but hoping for a spectacle, the African American elite from sea to sea turned out for the memorial service and burial of Penelope Lafayette St. James. It was held at the now infamous Virginia estate, as the late Mrs. St. James requested, and was the social event of the decade. As longtime associates of the Lafayette family, even Francine's parents had attended.

"Ursula St. James do you need a hug?" was all Francine could think to say, partly serious and partly in attempt to bring levity to her revelation.

"YES!" Ursula said, shaking her head matter-of-factly. They hugged like family and laughed incredulously.

The two topped off their day at Francine's place over a bottle of Riesling purchased for the occasion, AKA free dinner courtesy of the Ravencrest Welcome Reception. Ursula was so eager to confide in her newfound but familiar friend. She explained the rest of the story—that her father and cousin agreed to hastily and quietly transfer the deed of the Virginia estate to Ursula, whom they both loved almost as much as real estate. Unable to bring herself to visit the estate since the funeral, Ursula decided to set aside the matter until she could establish her career on her own dime. Her parents funded her degrees, but she needed to do the rest on her own—away from both sides of her family and their friends. The estate was in the hands of a lucky caretaker until she decided otherwise.

Francine shared that her parents, far less loaded than Ursula's, had decided she and her sister were tragically entitled and that they'd have to make something of themselves in their chosen careers. Francine and Ursula both confessed feeling simultaneously bound and freed by their newfound financial independence.

The two become confidantes over the next month of free meals. Francine would share her insecurity about her part-time status and regret over choosing passion over practicality in her studies. Once the semester got underway and they received regular pay, they replaced their free meals with biweekly lunches at the faculty dining room. Ursula always paid. It turned out, the Fortley family was the silent donor of the dining room and shared a similar colonial reputation as the St. Jameses. Upon learning of Ursula's new position at Ravencrest, the elderly Isola Fortley summoned her for tea. Mrs. Fortley had been a close friend of Ursula's grandmother, Fleurette St. James at the University of Pennsylvania and shared many confidences with the woman over the years in letters before Fleurette died delivering Ursula's aunt, Rose. Ursula recalled Aunt Rose's seasonal visits to Philadelphia but vaguely remembered any mention of with whom she spent time there. Cherishing the kinship she shared with the St. James women over the generations, Ursula St. James' money was no good at the Fortley-funded dining hall. The only caveat was that she dined with a friend.

"Friendship is essential, my dear Dr. Ursula," Mrs. Fortley had said once as they hugged goodbye. Ursula understood, finally. Mrs. Fortley knew her mother. She also knew that her mother wrestled with something that she could never quite put her finger on and refused to have someone else diagnose. Though unspoken, Ursula knew her mother's illness was part loneliness and depression. Despite being a respected high-profile socialite, the elder St. James counted among her peers no true friends even up to her death.

So it was settled. Ursula, with her friend, Francine, would dine at The Hibiscus Suite twice a month as the perpetual "guests cart blanche" of Mrs. Isola Fortley.

5

Francine moaned loudly, stirring awake the solid mass of delicious, brown arms and legs that lay beside her.

"What's wrong, baby?" Garrison said, sleep still hanging onto his words.

Francine moaned again, this time louder. "Could you pleeease rub my legs for me?"

If the smirk on his face implied to Francine how he interpreted her request, his quick dive underneath the covers confirmed it.

"I most certainly will, Love." His muffled voice called out.

Despite her pain, Francine couldn't help but to smile. No one could ever say he wasn't always ready to please.

"Nooooo, not like that, Nasty!"

Garrison's thick mane, wide, strong forehead, and confused eyes popped out from under the wrinkled, gold sheets.

"I don't understand," he said.

Francine rolled her eyes. "You *know*."

His face opened with comprehension.

"You're in pain?"

"Yes," she said, gritting her teeth.

"How long this time?"

Francine shrugged. She hated talking about it. She often wished she'd never told him; that she hadn't revealed what she viewed as her weakness; her thorn.

"No, for real, Frankie. How long?"

"Since yesterday."

Garrison shook his head. "That's a long time for a flare, right?"

She shrugged again and stared at the ceiling.

"Have you taken your meds?

She ignored him. "Could you please just massage them?"

Under the covers, Garrison repositioned himself on his side so that at least one hand was free to work the muscles in her thighs and calves.

Another moan escaped Francine's lips, this time one of relief.

"So, you are still too stubborn to take any medicine for it?"

She sighed.

"The meds just make me loopy. Fibromyalgia is not MS or anything. It's not progressive. It's not going to get worse unless I stop working out, eating right, or whatever. The last thing I want is to be dependent on medication. I just have to deal with it."

She was rambling, and she knew it.

"But how are you going to manage the pain?" he pressed.

"Well, Ursula was telling me about acupuncture …"

"Ursula! Oh God," Garrison shouted, cutting her off. He'd stopped massaging her and turned to lie on his back.

Francine stared at him for a few seconds. "Hey, what's up with you and her? Why don't you like her?"

"It's not that I don't like her. There's just something about the way everyone just defers to her. If I didn't know better, I'd think they were secretly bowing down to her in worship."

Francine chuckled loudly. A little too loudly.

"I'm serious, Frankie! I don't get it. Plus, with all the cuts and drama going on this week, folks are sincerely nervous and yet, she walks around so … so … unaffected."

It was amazing to Francine that Garrison didn't know who Ursula was. Maybe he just hadn't put two and two together yet? It was another confirmation for her of just how out of touch he was when it came to anything that had to do with culture and history—two things Francine lived and breathed. The truth was the truth, though. Ursula would not be affected by the recent budget cuts. She was connected even when she didn't want to be. Francine suspected she reminded Garrison of the status that eluded him in his last relationship.

"Oh," she said. She didn't have the strength to argue with him.

Over the last week, news had come from the president's office announcing that several departments at Ravencrest would have their budgets sliced and diced. Those departments included both Francine's (humanities and social sciences) and Garrison's (engineering). The good news was that Garrison's position was safe because his salary was funded by a grant and Francine's was safe simply because she was an adjunct who'd been around a while and well, adjuncts made up 70% of the teaching staff. The bad news was that the availability of research dollars—particularly important to Garrison's work—was nil.

"Now my arms." Francine tried to lift her arms up but they were heavy with pain and stiffness.

Garrison returned to his side. He took his thumb and pressed it into her tricep, held it for a minute, and then released it. It was an acupressure technique Francine had taught him when she first told him about fibro. That was years ago, and she could safely say that he'd mastered how to hit her spot.

In more ways than one, she thought and then giggled.

"What's so funny?" he said as he moved his thumb press to her wrist.

"Oh nothing," she smiled as she breathed deeply, attempting to push the pain out through her nose like she'd learned in one of the thousands of YouTube videos she'd watched on pain management.

Francine dreaded the next few hours when, after the pain of the flare would die down, chronic fatigue would settle into her body. Not to mention the restless sleep. She shook her head as if she could shake out the pending suffering.

"Anyway, I've heard from more than just Ursula that acupuncture is a great pain management technique."

Garrison started on her next arm. "Yeah, but you know what the problem will be, right?"

"Umm, no. The needles?"

Garrison shakes his head. “Nah, I heard you can’t even really feel them.”

Francine was relieved to hear that. She was secretly anxious about that part.

“What then?”

Garrison stops pressing her arm and stares at her intently.

“The cost. How are you going to pay for it?”

Francine turned her head away and pretended to deeply examine the wall on her side of the room. She didn’t want to ask him for the money. He’d already done so much for her by helping out with groceries and kicking in occasionally with the rent when she was short.

“I got another job,” she said whispering.

“Ohhhh! That’s riiiight.” He gently laid her arm down at her side and flipped back onto his back.

“Freaking the freakazoids!”

Francine, with the little strength she had, reached over and pinched his upper thigh.

“Ow! What? I’m just saying …” he said laughing. “… that’s what you do, right?”

“You don’t know what I do,” Francine mumbled, her mood permanently shifted. As much as she adored their lovemaking, she wanted him to go. Immediately. She had only a couple of hours before she had to be on the line and she wanted … needed … time to soak in some Epsom salts before her shift.

Interestingly, Francine didn’t quite know how to ask him to leave. She’d never done it before. She wasn’t sure if she’d ever wanted him to before. But there was something about the way he mocked her that triggered her courage.

“I have to get ready for work.” Her voice was even and resolute.

He didn’t get it.

Garrison looked at her and smirked in the way he usually did before their more inventive encounters.

"I can help you with that, you know. One more for the road?" He leaned into her, nuzzling his face in her neck and kissing her nape.

She pushed him off. "Really, dude?"

"I know, I know," he said as he reluctantly rose into a seated position on the bed. "You're in 'pain.'" He made finger quotes with his hands.

Pain and all, Francine shot up and out of the bed.

"What the hell was that about?!" She mimicked his air quotes.

Garrison appeared to be a little shocked by her visceral reaction to his pseudo-joke.

"Well, I have to admit, Frankie. The strange thing about fibro is … well, no one can tell you're sick. You look fine. You certainly don't look like you're in pain."

Rage filled Francine. "Oh, so because I don't look sick, that means I'm not? What … you think I'm making this up or something?"

Garrison's eyes bulged. He'd never intended to upset her so much. But he found her response intriguing. It was like another layer had been peeled back by his inadvertent challenge.

"Of course not. I don't think that at all."

He could feel the heat from her.

"I don't know. It's like the silent killer or something."

Francine throws her hands into the air, exasperated. "Killer? Really?!"

Francine threw the decorative bed pillows that had been strewn across the floor during their rendezvous. When the pillows proved ineffective, she moved on to pile of shoes that were next to her bed.

Flip-flop to the shoulder.

Slipper to the back of the head.

When she lifted up a stiletto, Garrison raised his hands, "No, no, no, Frankie! That was a poor choice of words! Stop!"

Francine stopped and stared at him. He was a lovely man. As physically beautiful as anyone she'd ever seen. His arms were chiseled better than any statue in Rome. And he was certainly brilliant. Had a mind that dazzled her with the expanse of his knowledge and the books he'd read. But there were days like this one, that felt like neon signs glaring at her, demanding that she hold back the entirety of her heart from him.

Garrison walked over to Francine and held her. Her anger had exhausted her and she leaned against him even though she didn't want to.

"It's just that you do so much for someone who is in pain all the time. I worry about you."

Francine could only muster one word. "Don't."

She didn't have the energy to explain to him why she had to keep going; why she did so much; why she couldn't stop. He'd only ask, "What's so bad about stopping every now again?" This would reveal his ignorance about the illness and would only frustrate her more—since that would mean he hadn't bothered to take the time to learn a little about what ails her. She'd had this same conversation over and over again with every guy she'd dated seriously, and it was always the same. She was done talking about it. No one could really understand fibromyalgia unless they suffered from it themselves, so why bother? It was her burden. Hers and hers alone. As always, she'd continue to push past the pain and only take her meds when it was absolutely necessary. Considering the fact that her arms felt like smoldering coal under her skin in that moment, she'd definitely have to pop a couple of muscle relaxers before starting work.

Francine considered calling in but reminded herself about the costs of acupuncture and decided against it. Her "freakazoids" were just going to get a woozy Zora that night.

***

Francine was diagnosed with fibromyalgia almost a decade prior, as an undergrad. It was actually not long after the traumatic encounter with her roommate's boyfriend. For six months straight, Francine experienced extreme pain all over her body, had trouble sleeping, and found herself dragging with exhaustion throughout the day. Thinking that she just had a bug she couldn't shake, Francine went to the campus clinic. The doctor there referred her to a rheumatologist at Hampton General. After eliminating much more serious autoimmune diseases, she was formally diagnosed with fibromyalgia and told that she would need to take pain meds to manage it. With the first round of medication, Francine experienced awful hallucinations, night terrors that would send her heart racing and keep her from sleeping for days out of fear. With the second round, she'd had light shocks in her head and floating objects in her vision. At that point, she decided she would rather go without meds than deal with the crazy side effects. Her remedies, temporary as they were: nutrition, exercise, holistic treatments, and the occasional muscle relaxer like Valium or Flexeril. Oh … and staying busy. She determined that she could never, ever stop long enough to think about the illness, much less allow it to consume her life.

While there isn't much information about what causes fibro, there are a number of reputable theories. Some studies say that the neurological syndrome comes from a kind of post-traumatic stress syndrome, that something occurs in the brain of people who experience PTSD that decreases their tolerance to pain and increases other sensitivities. But even these theories are inconclusive. Francine refused to blame her roommate or what happened to her for her diagnosis. It was her "thorn," and she accepted it. Since being diagnosed, Francine had obtained a master's degree, a Ph.D., and traveled extensively. At least on paper, she'd accomplished a lot. So in a way, the constant presence of fibro was a reminder of how capable she was of overcoming anything.

***

"You alright, Zora?" the monitor called out to Francine, snapping her out of la la land. "You seem a little spacey tonight."

"I'm okay," Zora said.

"Step. Away. From. The. Wine," the monitor said with a chuckle.

Zora laughed herself. "Nope, no wine tonight. Just had a long day."

"Yeah, okay," the monitor said sarcastically.

A few minutes went by as she waited for her next call.

"Well, looks like your night is about to get a little longer," the monitor said.

"What do you mean?"

"Got your boyfriend on the line."

"Wait … what?"

Francine had zoned out again. She was thinking about Garrison and his earlier insensitivity, so when the monitor said "boyfriend," she was confused. Why would he be calling the line?

"You know! Chase."

"Ohhhh. Okay. Send him through."

As much as she preferred to not talk to Chase when she was so out of it, she felt like she needed something different. And he was certainly that.

"Hey, you," she said as she put on her slippers and relaxed back on the papasan chair in her tiny living room.

"Tire suas roupas agora!"

Francine sat up quickly.

"Woah, *Amante*! You're getting right to the action tonight, huh? I like it, baby. Tops or bottoms?"

Chase's role-plays were always fun. Cultured, even. She figured he was playing the Portuguese conquistador or something. She would be his latest conquest. But her enthusiasm was met with silence.

"Hello?"

More silence.

"Chase?"

"*Cale a boca e fazer o que eu disse!* Now!"

His harshness startled her. He'd always been soft spoken and kind. Even in his role-plays. But this was something else. Darker. Definitely not their usual. Often, their conversations veered away from sex and into more interesting discussions of current events, literature, and culture. That was right up her alley. He seemed to be both a well-read and well-traveled man, and they often spoke to each other in the many languages they were both fluent in. Francine looked forward to his calls as they were a welcomed break from all the horny guys who called in. But, for sure, if he wanted to switch things up, she was more than capable of treating him just like the rest of them. Starting with a prompt cursing out.

Francine railed him in Portuguese. She wanted to let him know that she didn't appreciate his change in demeanor but didn't want to trigger an interception by the monitor.

"Pára de falar e fazer o que eu disse!"

It was low. Barely audible. But she heard it. She heard the slight sniffle and immediately felt bad about her reaction. Technically, he *was* paying for the call and could say whatever he wanted. She certainly wasn't trying to make the man cry.

"Are you okay, Chase?"

"I'm so sorry, Zora. I really am. I have a lot going on right now. And I guess I'm just taking my frustrations … the pressure … out on you. You don't deserve that."

His voice returned to its low raspy, rumble.

"Stuff at work?" Francine probed.

"Yes. I had to let some people go, people who have been with us for a long time. It wasn't pretty."

"Oh man. That's pretty tough. Restructuring?"

Chase didn't say anything at first. Francine had always imagined that he worked in mergers and acquisitions for some big accounting or consulting firm. Whatever he did, she was sure he was in a position of power based on the way he spoke about his team and the people they served.

"Yeah, something like that. You know how it is. When the money runs out …"

Francine finished his sentence, "—something gets cut. Yeah, I've been observing something similar in my other life, too. Seems like that's going around nowadays."

She got the sense from him that he wanted to talk more. That he needed to vent. To release. Wasn't that what most of the men called in to do in one form or the other anyway? But it was getting close to the 20-minute mark and he'd never stayed over into her bonus minutes before.

"You know, Chase, if you'd like to talk more, I'm here for you. If you need to yell or scream or …" she tread lightly with the last one "… cry, you can do that with me. This is a safe…"

"I can't, Z. I wish I could but I can't. I gotta go. Talk soon."

The line went dead. Nineteen minutes and 53 seconds.

The next voice Francine heard was the monitor.

"Whew! Intense."

"No kidding," Francine said.

"Oh yeah," the monitor continued. "Can't cuss the clients out in other languages either, okay?"

Francine smiled, though her mind still lingered on her lonely friend.

6

The next morning, Francine still felt tired. Not so much from the pain but from the treadmill of her stagnant racing around. From classes to meetings to the late-night gig and dates with G, it was a little much. Staring at herself in the mirror, she made a decision. Francine wiped the night from her face as if removing a vaudeville mask. This is not who she had sacrificed to become. She hated to admit it, but it was the liberating truth: She was better, smarter than she had been conducting herself.

Francine walked into the main room of her apartment, pulled out her journal, and wrote out her declarations.

There were three:

#1. Invest time and energy on professional development and branding.

This meant more time pursuing the right opportunities, specifically strategic fellowship applications, a post-doc maybe, casual networking with university brass, broadening the social-professional circle. She had initiated productive appointments with Ursula and Dean Mercer to discuss specific opportunities.

#2. Find a second job that related to her aspirations in some way.

This meant quitting NTS. She had done so gracefully and even had a long farewell conversation with Chase, who said he was proud of her and wished her the best. He even went over his time allotment to listen as she, for a change, did most of the talking. It *was* time to quit.

Francine found work tending bar at a four-star hotel in town during the happy hour shift of 4-7 p.m. The tips were great, the hours were perfect, and the clientele was appreciative of her attention to their need for confidentiality, full glasses, and intelligent conversation. In return, she was able to broaden her social professional circle.

#3. Redirect emotional energy to numbers 1 and 2.

Time with Garrison had to include discussions and resources related to these pursuits. She needed to utilize every relationship she had to achieve her goals. Like it or not, Garrison was good at getting what he wanted. She could learn a few things from him in that department. She would think of him as a consultant. Thankfully, Garrison admired her focus shift and took his role as consultant seriously. Francine was happy to have a created a context (rather, a box with a lid) for his advice.

A month later, Francine felt great about the way the changes made her feel but also was slightly ambivalent about the decisions specifically. On one hand, she was proud of her renewed clarity and purpose. On the other, she felt embarrassed by what she now saw as frivolity in the way she had been conducting her life up until that point.

But she was making progress and that's what mattered. She met with Ursula to touch up on her power politics. Life on the fringes of the elite allowed Francine to "forget" some of the realities of polite, high-stakes competition. She needed one of these opportunities to come through, and if anyone could help her get the edge on the nuances of submitting winning applications, it was Ursula. Francine was already excellent at following instructions and reading underlying preferences. Ursula was happy to help by offering insightful background on the respective boards, committees, and sensitivities behind the granting agencies that worked to inform Francine's choices for references and phrasing around strategic initiatives.

The meeting with Dean Roseline Mercer proved even more intriguing. Francine initially asked to meet with Roseline to talk about the Sherman Fellowship and gain her endorsement and hopefully a letter of reference. Also, she wanted to ask how winning the grant would impact her return to campus, preferably full time. Roseline listened to Francine's pitch attentively over a steaming aroma of tea—an exotic blend, no doubt. Roseline, like Francine's mother, was one of those people who could drink hot tea or soup all year around. She paused, looking intently at Francine, for what seemed like the longest five seconds ever. Then, she took another sip of the steaming aromatic herbal beverage. Francine kept a stiff spine, determined to appear confident. Roseline stood up and walked around the long, solid teak claw-foot desk to the mantle over the antique fireplace that had been refaced with beautiful Andalusian tiles. She handed Francine a postcard that she took from a small crystal letter tray. It announced an award competition sponsored by WHUP, the prestigious women's organization responsible for Roseline's claim to fame. Apparently, they offered an invitation-only grant. Francine had never heard of it.

"Is this a new award?" she asked.

Roseline responded without directly answering Francine's question, "The Search Fellowship invites scholars who demonstrate promise in human-centered leadership in higher education. Interviews will be held next month, so submit your application at least a week ahead of time. The applicant pool is very small and extremely selective. Everything is on the website. Use my name to login. Your password instructions will be sent via email. I'll have Noah schedule you for a few meetings between now and then to check your progress. Make sure he has your availability. Good luck, Dr. Carty."

Somehow during Roseline's recitation, she managed to walk Francine to the door. Smooth or rude, Francine wasn't sure. Maybe both. They were now standing at Noah's desk.

Francine stood staring at the back of the embossed card. It read simply: The Search. The web address was centered in the same font underneath. Francine cleared her throat, trying to look nonplused, "Thank you Ros—Dean Mercer."

"You're welcome, Francine. Noah will take it from here. Noah?" she made the transaction with a smile.

"Um. Hi, Noah," she uttered.

"Dr. Carty. Looks as if we need to get you set up for a few appointments!"

***

This called for an emergency debriefing with Ursula. As usual, Francine sat on the impeccably tufted grey bench in the foyer of The Hibiscus Suite waiting for Ursula to come trotting up the stairs, precisely five minutes tardy. Her workouts paying off, Ursula appeared less winded than previous months, "Dr. Francine Carty, what gives? This is an unexpected treat."

"Yessss. Please sit." Francine followed the host in the grey blazer to the table she requested when she arrived.

"This must be juicy. You have us back in the corner, in the shadows! What's going on?" Ursula plied.

Francine recounted the meeting with Dean Mercer in hushed tones, feeling nervous, excited, and a little ridiculous. Ursula listened, sipping her lime seltzer though a straw almost without a breath. When Francine finished the recap. Ursula looked at her incredulously.

"What?!" Francine insisted.

"I wasn't sure it actually existed and it falls—plop—right into your lap! Unbelievable," Ursula said in a whisper.

"What does that mean?!" Francine was pulled into Ursula's mysterious reaction.

"Let me see it! Do you have it? Can I see it? No, not here." Ursula asked.

"Ursula! Get a hold of yourself! Take another sip and calm down," Francine chastised. "How are you going to help *me* if *you're* all unraveled and hysterical? I need to hear everything you know. Is this that big of a deal? I've never heard of it."

"Okay, I'm being a little ridiculous. You know I'm a groupie when it comes to this kind of thing," Ursula exhaled a little.

Over hushed tones at what they often called The Isola Fortley Friendship Table at The Hibiscus Suite, Ursula informed Francine that the award was an elusive prize administered by a private group of WHUP members and supported by a powerful network women from around the world, most of whom were unnamed publicly. Candidates apply by invitation only and are interviewed in person by members of the committee. Roseline Mercer used a considerable amount of her settlement to endow the award, which has been matched by likeminded women and friends throughout academia. The criteria are unknown until the invitation is extended, when it is extended, which is whenever a candidate is identified. It was the real reason why Ursula applied for the position at Ravencrest. Not because she necessarily wanted or needed the prize but for its mystique and because Roseline Mercer, its founder, was there.

Awestruck, Francine couldn't believe she had never heard of this or that Roseline Mercer had extended the invitation to her. What had *she* done to warrant the invitation? She didn't want to ask, but she had to figure it out: Did *The Search* invitation mean Roseline would not be writing her a letter for the Sherman Fellowship application?

Later that day, Garrison sat at the bar where Francine's worked, similarly summoned to decipher the invitation to apply for The Search. His reaction incensed her. He began by revealing that the princess trophy ex's mom is a big wig in WHUP and a contributor to the award. Francine's felt the slow, quiet burn. She was green.

"Good luck. No one really knows what it takes to garner an invitation, but apparently you've got that *je ne sais quoi*," he prattled on.

Francine didn't hear much else he said for the time he remained. She wiped the mahogany counter in a circular motion, subconsciously rubbing away the resentment she felt for the esteem he held for this family who rejected him. She wondered if that was *why* he loved the princess. If so, did he see himself slumming it with her? Francine tried to compartmentalize her resentment of his ex, ignorance about The Search, and her feelings for Garrison. She poured herself a shot of Hennessy with lemon and placed it by the register.

***

Francine spent the next few weeks working on both applications—The Sherman Fellowship and The Search—from dawn until she needed to shower for class. The applications seemed simple but were actually torture. They asked big questions but required a maximum response of one page. Fortunately, it was the kind of torture that Francine relished. She would write, get better ideas in the shower, then jot down edit notes for later. Francine often found herself mumbling phrases and thoughts aloud. She was becoming a nutty professor before her very own eyes! After two weeks, she had close to her final drafts and was anxious to share them for feedback.

The meetings with Roseline proved helpful in an unexpected way. She'd clearly read over the drafts in advance, handing the marked-up copies over to Francine at the close of their meeting. Instead of directly discussing the application in the meeting, Roseline would ask a series of seemingly tangential questions about her life choices, the influence of her personal background and experiences on her career aspirations, fears, friends, and life at Ravencrest. Her questions were surprisingly intrusive but absolutely sincere. Francine felt inexplicably compelled to answer as if her life were an open book. She often wondered if her meetings with Roseline were how therapy felt. Each night afterward, Francine would drive home and watch the Brene Brown TED talk she'd seen on vulnerability to reaffirm her openness as a good thing. A day or so later, Francine would realize her responses to Roseline's questions were indeed related, critical in fact, to The Search application and maybe the Sherman, too. Then she'd spend an hour revising her *latest* perfect draft.

Just as Francine was reaching the point of fatigue, the applications grew legs. Her letters of reference for the Sherman all came in within a 72-hour timeframe, including one from Roseline. She received an email with the time and date of The Search interview, or "conversation," as it was noted in the message. In a fit of reckless abandon, Francine asked Garrison *and* Ursula to meet at her place to comb through her application and prepare for the conversation. She hoped Garrison would set aside his envy of Ursula for the occasion and hoped Ursula's "keys-to-the-kingdom" didn't jingle too loudly.

"If I can pull this off, maybe I have a future in ego management," Francine said aloud as she tapped send.

"Or storm watching."

As luck would have it, both Garrison and Ursula were pretty preoccupied with their own workloads. But they agreed to come over to perform the triage at 7 p.m. in exchange for dinner. They arrived at the same time.

Why can't we all just get along, Francine thought, as she rushed them into her place fearful of what damage might result by leaving them alone for too long.

"Thank you so much for carving time for this at such a critical time in the semester," she said as she greeted them with hugs. "I promise, this won't take long. I have specific things I need your input on ..."

She delegated responsibilities as she heaped their plates full of curried chicken, rice, cabbage, and plantains.

Garrison gave her a look that said, "You had better feed me for this."

Ursula effused over the reception in a way that said, "I appreciate your acknowledgement of placing me in this situation and I accept your recompense. That said, I *might* behave myself as I perform my duty."

These two.

Grateful, Francine said grace over the food and they got down to business.

An hour and a half later, Ursula had done exactly what she said she would. She'd reviewed Francine's written materials for appropriate tone, indirect cultural/social references, and inventoried her friend's closet for an ensemble and accessories that made the right statement. Garrison had helped by making sure she mined every detail for a winning grant proposal and rehearsed the interview. He and Ursula took turns giving feedback on her body language.

She was ready.

"You're going to get this," Ursula whispered in her ear as she hugged Francine on her way out. "You have to! I'm dying of curiosity!" The two women laughed as Ursula made her way down the concrete path that led to the driveway.

Francine leaned against the door as she locked it. Garrison stayed behind to pour her the last of the bottle of wine he'd brought over.

"Garrison, I love you. You take such good care of me." She took the wine glass from him and set it down on the counter. She wrapped her arms around his neck and plunged into a kiss. "Can you stay for a bit?" she asked looking into his eyes.

He returned a hungry kiss that said, "Was I busy? Nah, that data *will* analyze itself!" In what seemed like expert choreography, he hoisted her thighs around his waist, her fluffy purple slippers falling from her feet to the floor as he carried her to the bedroom.

***

Francine got an early start the next morning. Garrison had left at the crack of dawn to workout and head over to his lab. She, on the other hand, figured she'd set aside time later that night for grading the last of her classes' papers and submitting their midterm grades. Because of all the burning of midnight oil she did getting the applications together, much of her work for classes had shifted to weekends. This meant that she would have to check in back home and get out for errands a little earlier in the day. That week, Francine skimped on groceries and wine in order to afford a professional gel manicure. A visit to the hair salon was out of the question, but she thanked God that she was wearing her hair short. A stop at Hairtrix Discount Beauty Mart would have to do. She could get a premium leave-in moisturizer there for under $10.

Francine dialed her parents while she relaxed in a warm bubble bath.

"Good morning. Carty residence," an unexpected voice greeted her.

Splashing, Francine sat up in the tub abruptly, "Robbi!? What are you doing home?"

"That's *Specialist Robena Carty*, baby sister," she announced. The sisters shrieked in unison.

"Congratulations! I knew you would get it!" the younger Carty sister beamed. "Where to now? Is that why you're home? Why didn't you *tell* me you were coming?!"

"Botswana. Yes, this is my celebratory vacation. I wanted to surprise everyone. And before you ask, I just got in last night and will be here for two weeks," Robena answered in her best official tone.

Frankie heard her father in the background, "That's right. Foreign Service *Specialist* Carty in the *house*! You have a uniform or something *official* you can wear to the Faulkner funeral this afternoon?"

"Not since the 19th century, Dad," Robena laughed..

Her mother chimed in in the background, "Let the child get some rest. I have plenty for her to do later. She gon' help me do these heads tonight, right baby?" Is that Frankie? Is she coming home? Hi Frankie, talk later!"

"Oooh Robbi, call me later. Mommy gon' have you doing dead heads' hair and makeup. Sorry girl. You should have come up here first! They're going to work you like a Mississippi slave!" Frankie laughed as she continued, "I have so much to tell you. I'll call you on the sister line when I finish grading. It'll be late."

Their parents kept the second telephone line on in the girls' old room from when the girls were teenagers. Even though they had a house large enough for Robena and Francine to have separate rooms, they always shared the large guest suite on the third floor. Guests would use the bedrooms and baths on the second floor. Though four years apart, the two girls had always been very close. Sharing a room was definitely part of it.

"That's perfect. I'm still a little jet lagged from Dubai. I'll be wide-awake. I think I will go to the funeral. You know the Faulkners kept things interesting, something juicy might happen. Plus, it'll give me a chance to see everybody in one place."

"You're right about that. It's so good to have you stateside," Frankie whined.

"It's good to be home. Okay. Get your work done. We're long overdue for a marathon catch-up. You think you can get down here next weekend?" Robena asked.

"… Actually, I think so. You might have to rent me a car …" Francine laughed.

"If you can make the time, I'll get you here," Robena offered. "Just call me tonight."

"I will," Francine said, "And Robbi?"

"Yes?" Robbi asked.

"I'm so proud of you," Frankie beamed.

"Thanks, Franks," Robena replied knowingly. "Your due is coming, Doc."

"Ugghhhh. I'm working on it," Frankie replied. Her sister's telepathy was always impressive.

"I know you are. Chat with you tonight, Franks."

"Bye, Robs."

The Carty women were extremely capable and felt grateful for the more-than-comfortable upbringing and education their parents provided them. Still, it was a psychological and emotional struggle to meet the challenges and expectations their parents regularly set before them. Both women understood that it would build their fortitude to make their own way in the world, but the reality of that was not always easy. It was not as if Benjamin and Gwendolyn would actually let them starve or anything. But they all—the parents and the daughters—had too much pride to find themselves in the position of reneging on the deal early on: The girls would surely inherit the Carty business, home, and liquid assets, but beyond their undergraduate degrees, they would have to make their own ways in the world. And pride mattered.

Francine finished her bath, completed her moisture-maximus grooming routine and got dressed for her Saturday morning errands. Reflecting on yesterday's triage consult with Garrison and Ursula, she chose a pair of denim trousers and a black wool turtleneck for her errands. She dug for her black loafers and slipped a black leather belt with a vintage silver clasp through the loops. Small antique-finished hoops were always appropriate. A sweep of gloss on her lips and two strokes of mascara completed her look. Casual professional. *You never know who you'll run into out in the street*, Francine recalled her mother's mantra as she slipped on the white, down puffer vest she got for Christmas last year and snapped a photo of the grocery list on her kitchen chalkboard with her phone.

"Alright, let's get it!" she said to herself as she headed to her car, which had been running uncharacteristically well these days.

Francine clipped her phone into a hands-free holster on the dash and called her friend Comfort on speaker while she started the car.

"I knew I would hear from you today!" Comfort answered.

"Well, hello to you too!" Francine responded laughing.

"You know your parents have the Faulkner funeral? Everybody is going to be there, and by everybody, I mean your ex-boyfriend, my ex-husband, the man I *should* have married, and his crazy fiancée," Comfort announced.

"That is precisely why I *won't* be there," Francine said checking behind her as she worked her car out of the tight parking space. "I can't even afford drama. And I mean that in every possible way."

"Well, zen lady, you might want to reconsider. Didn't *His Hotness* used to date the dearly departed Rev. Faulkner's daughter?" Comfort really knew how to stir a pot, using her pet name for Garrison.

"*His Hotness* dated the daughter of a close family friend of the late reverend. You love starting trouble, Comfort."

"Friend of the family, I'm sure! He was also that girl's daddy."

"Whaaaaattt???" Francine stopped at the yellow light she frequently ignored.

"Yessss."

"No!"

"Yes. You know my Auntie worked for Judge Hairston forever. The crypt keeper, they called him. Everybody went to the judge to document and confidentially care for the secrets they wanted taken to the grave," Comfort was just warming up.

"I don't believe it," Frankie tried not to inhale the salacious dirt on Garrison's Princess Patrice. It didn't work.

Comfort laid out the story. "DNA don't lie, my friend. Apparently, the good reverend got carried away with the laying on of the hands. The mom was wayward as a young girl, you know. She spent the summer down here with relatives from time to time. So the grandparents sent the girl overseas for a while. When she came back to the States, she had a baby *and* a husband. You know how it goes, a richy-rich investment banker who was age appropriate. They were set up real nice in Manhattan. Good man, Mr. Dallas Lashley. He raised up Princess Patti, just like she was his own. Investing the reverend's money 'til the reverend, too, become richy rich—on TOP of the money that the Church of the High Hill Tabernacle rakes in. That, my sister, is the story of the precious princess, Patrice *Faulkner* Lashley."

"I don't know what to say …" Francine said, reeling with the new information. "That's kind of sad. I've only met her once, kind of."

"Yes, as you were putting the moves on *His Hotness* in ya dirty red sneaks. Hmph! Now ya wan' be sad for her?" Comfort set the record straight.

"ANYWAY," Francine interrupted. "I've always resented Garrison's adoration of her or rather, her family's standing. And now all along, she's at the center of this awful, terrible scandal. It's a shame. I actually think I don't hate her anymore."

"Well, hate her or not, you need to check in with your man to see if he's planning a trip to the Big Apple. I'll do the watching down here," Comfort waited for Francine to agree.

"Oh, Comfort! I really can't think about this right now! I have my interview, conversation, whatever it is, Tuesday and I need to focus," Francine said.

"That's right, your mystery moneybag for travel. Good luck!" Comfort followed Francine's lead in exiting from the Faulkner saga.

"Oh, but I'm trying to come down this weekend. Robbi's home!"

"Secret Squirrel?" Comfort exclaimed. "Fantastic!"

"You know she hates when you call her that," Francine warned.

"I know she does. And I hate that she stole Ricky Ray from me. He was the cutest boy in the 5th grade, and I snagged him," Comfort began. Francine chimed in to finish the tale in unison, "Then, here comes Robbi longlegs, in that snake-skinned, denim miniskirt. Ricky Ray couldn't even remember my *name*!" The friends laughed out loud.

"Seriously, she got her promotion to specialist and will be stationed in Botswana," Francine said proudly.

"Wow! She is really doing her thing. She'll be an ambassador before we know it," Comfort said seriously, shifting into King's English.

"That's her plan. In the meantime, I hope she'll be in Botswana long enough for me to get a job that will allow me to afford to visit her there," Francine hoped.

"It'll come. Good luck on your interview. Call me Tuesday night. I'll save my report from the funeral until then." Francine loved her girl. Comfort was always on the job.

Tapping the end icon on her phone, Francine got out of the car. She had been parked the last few minutes of her conversation with Comfort. It was still early, but the nail salon was already full. Nevertheless, she signed in for her service and took a seat. She had a place in West Philly, Roxborough, and Chestnut Hill for nails, but because this was for a special occasion and she had other errands to run, she chose the salon on Germantown Avenue in Chestnut Hill. The nail techs were good, and the atmosphere was relaxing. It was also across the street from an artisan bakery and half a mile from Hairtrix, her favorite beauty supply store that kept in stock all of the best hair products. An added benefit? Her apartment in Mt. Airy was just a short drive away.

One of her regular spots, the one in West Philly, was funky and colorful and owned by a young African American who was committed to revitalizing the Powelton Village commercial district adjacent to the University City neighborhood that was gentrified in the 1990s, largely by University of Pennsylvania. Francine loved to support small, black business owners, and it didn't hurt that Lancaster Avenue had some great eclectic spots—boutiques and such—that were taking great advantage of their proximity to the University City commercial district. But today, she had to stay on schedule, which meant close to home.

The receptionist motioned to Francine to take a seat at the open desk. Forty minutes later, her nails were cleaned, cut, buffed, shaped, and gleaming with a fresh coat of get-the-job neutral gel enamel. Satisfied that her manicure was perfect, Francine went about her way to complete her remaining errands. As soon as she got into the car, the phone vibrated. Ursula's name showed up. Francine flipped the ringer back on and answered the call on speaker. "Good morning, Miz St. James."

"Cut it out," Ursula replied. "Guess who just called me and invited *us* to dessert and tea, Sunday afternoon at 4?"

"Who?"

"Mrs. Isola Fortley, that's who!" Ursula stated nervously.

"Did we do something wrong? Should I have gone over or called to thank her for being your plus one at The Hibiscus Suite?" Francine panicked.

"I don't think so. I'm not sure she even knows who I bring. What am I saying, of course she knows. She's Isola Fortley," Ursula spoke rapidly. "I don't know what she wants, and I didn't ask. I just said, 'Yes ma'am, Dr. Francine Carty and I graciously accept your invitation.' Can you make it? You have to come with me."

"Are you kidding? How could I not? Thank God I just had my nails done. What do we wear to see her? What does she want? She asked for me by name?!"

"She did indeed. Are you going to church?" Ursula was reading her mind.

"Of course. I'm going to need prayer! There's no way I'm making it though this week without a word. Can you drive?"

"I'll pick you up at 10:45. Maybe we can grab a bite before heading out to Mrs. Fortley's."

Francine spent the rest of the day running on adrenaline as she mowed through errands and student work, beating her midnight deadline to submit grades. She pulled out of her closet a modest couture dress from her previous life when her parents kept accounts for her and Robena at Saks, Neiman's, and Nordstrom.

"We always represent the family business. You must dress properly in public!" their mother would remind them.

Gwendolyn "Winnie" Carty was a mistress of presentation. Unfortunately, that talent was lost on Francine. But she had committed the basics to memory. Still undecided about the first dress, Francine shifted the hangers of casual academia wear so she could survey the back of her closet—the Winnie Carty section, she called it, with each item on premium hangers in cloth garment bags. She finally selected an understated navy St. John dress that fell just below the knee. In a special-occasion jewelry chest she kept tucked away on the floor behind her snow boots, she chose a single strand of 15-inch pearls with matching earrings. On the top shelf of the closet, Francine reached for the shoebox that contained the pumps she saved for those Winnie and Bennie occasions. And on the very last two hangers of the closet, just beneath the shoebox, hung her steel grey cashmere belted coat and the ivory trench she brought with her from home—just in case. Francine, with deep conditioner seeping from the plastic cap on her head, found herself staring at upward of $20,000 in Winnie and Bennie classics in her closet.

Abruptly, she pulled the string to the fixtureless light bulb overhead. Standing in the darkness of the room, Francine felt a wave of emotions rush over her. In a teary blur, Francine messaged her sister:

> Frankie: *Really tired and feeling a bit overwhelmed. Call u in the a.m. Early. F*
>
> Robbi: *If you're okay to wait until a.m., I'm okay. R u ok?*
>
> Frankie: *Yeah, just a little bluesy. Long day, big week. Good night.*
>
> Robbi: *Early!*
>
> Frankie: *Yes, Spec. Carty ;)*

The next morning, Francine called Robena on the sister line and unloaded all of her woes: the inadequacy she felt professionally, the shame she harbored about having been a sex worker, the uneasiness she felt about letting herself go with Garrison, the ambivalence about the nature her financial situation, the frustration of her fibro, as well as the positive angst she was experiencing in her decision to set a new agenda for accomplishing her professional goals, and the pressure of everything happening at once—the Sherman Fellowship application submission, the "conversation" about The Search grant, and now the meeting with Mrs. Fortley. Robena listened as Francine let it all out. At the end of her 40-minute unraveling, Robena told her to check her email for an open-ended round trip flight home.

"Get your butt on a flight right after that interview. You're no good to anyone if you're not well. You need a break. Your students are probably burned out after midterms anyway," she said in big-sister mode. "Text me your flight information, and I'll come get you. We'll go straight for drinks from the airport before we come home. I won't tell Winnie and Bennie you're coming, so they won't make a fuss until they see you."

Francine thanked her big sister and agreed to her suggestions. "Let me get up so I can get ready for church. Lord knows I need it. Call you later?"

"For sure. I need to get up, too. You know the Cartys can't miss church. I told Bennie and Winnie they could sleep in before service. I'm going in to the office this morning. It'll be good to visit with everyone during the downtime. That Faulkner service was quite the spectacle. Your friend, Crazy Comfort, was in full effect. And you know the Cartys laid the good reverend out in style."

"We always do!" they laughed in unison.

"Enjoy tea with Lady Fortley. Take her some booze for her tea. Wasn't that your job when we worked the repasts?" Robena teased.

"Yes, indeed. Those mourners loved to see me coming with my 'tea' pot. That's what got me the bartending job at the Four Seasons Philadelphia!" Francine boasted. "You know what? That's actually a good idea. I have just enough time to mix her up a pint of Carty's special blend."

The talk with Robena did a world of good to lift Francine's spirits. She was impeccably presentable for church and tea. She carried with her the pint of Carty brew disguised nicely in a decorative monogrammed decanter and gift bag when Ursula arrived to pick her up for church.

Grace United Methodist Church was half full. Both Ursula and Francine liked worshipping there because of the whole *salt of the earth,* family atmosphere. Visiting churches was one of the things they did together from early on in their friendship. They had tried the prestigious mega-churches in Philadelphia but decided it best to decline the celebrity church vibe and the over-produced atmosphere that seemed inescapable. In light of both their circumstances, they agreed it would be best to fly under the radar at a church where the people were less likely to know or care about their backgrounds. While Francine certainly didn't have the lineage of Ursula, the Cartys were funeral royalty, so churches of significant size were sure to know the name. And well, Ursula just didn't want to be bothered with the who's who game that ensued when she encountered the black elite anywhere. Grace Church fit the bill. They were warmly greeted as frequent visitors and welcomed to participate as much or as little as they chose. It was a really nice family church.

Third Sundays were Francine's favorite because the children's choir sang. They had so much spirit, and the youngest of the kids, about 4 or 5 years old, always sang the loudest and swayed out of step with the choir. There was one little girl who couldn't have been older than 4, who often stole the spotlight and enjoyed every bit of it. She was quite the hamlette and sang her little heart out. Francine and Ursula recognized the child's mother, who beamed tearfully whenever the children sang, as an administrator at Ravencrest whom neither of them knew personally. The purity of the children's voices was the highlight of the service.

The older kids were also impressively active in the church. There were about 15 teenagers who were contenders as the best youth praise team in the city. They also ushered and assisted with recording the services. Francine learned leadership and responsibility in her family's business, but a lot of her peers learned those same characteristics in churches like Grace.

It was the second Sunday when Ursula and Francine visited before tea with Mrs. Fortley. The men's chorus was singing. Most of the men were senior citizens and as unabashed as the children in their worship. But there was something, too, about a men's chorus Francine loved. One of the most stirring and popular features of the Carty services was the a cappella men's quintet that sat amongst the mourners. When their voices rose, the crowd always looked around for the choir. Then one by one, the men would stand from wherever they were dispersed in the pews and walk to the front of the congregation. People were amazed that such a beautiful powerful sound came from just five voices. But the Cartys couldn't take credit for it. Ironically, her father said he and her mother first saw it at a funeral they attended in Philadelphia. The men were from a church chorus and were commissioned to perform at the funeral. Always about the business, Bennie and Winnie Carty's eyes locked in an aha moment whenever they spoke of when they started incorporating the quintet in their own services. The twist for them was that they auditioned and hired their own singers to replicate the experience.

After the service, Francine and Ursula greeted the familiar faces of the worshipers, including their colleague, the pastor, and the first lady. Then, they walked a couple of blocks to the neighborhood restaurant for a powwow about their summons. *Relish* was a full-service family restaurant owned by a pair of brothers who were proprietors of a number of successful establishments over the years: a nightclub on Broad Street where the city's current mayor once worked as the disc jockey, a jazz club in Center City, a blues supper club on the waterfront, an upscale fine-dining restaurant, an organic lunch spot, and a Parisian bistro in Chestnut Hill. *Relish*, in the West Oak Lane neighborhood, had been an anchor in reviving the commercial corridor of the community, which was hit hard by the 1980s crack cocaine epidemic. The neighbors, as well as influential politicians, worked very hard to restore the community's vitality as a stable and desirable environment for working-class homeowners.

To get down to business, both Francine and Ursula selected the brunch buffet. It was crowded, as usual. Francine shared her meltdown the day before with Ursula, as well as her plans to head home after the "conversation" as they worked their way around the buffet of downhome and uptown soul food favorites. Over what likely added up to a pitcher of mimosas, they decided that with all due respect, "Mrs. Fortley called the meeting, so Mrs. Fortley can worry about the meeting. Cheers to Lady Fortley!" they giggled. Still, they arrived bearing gifts: a fresh bouquet and the Carty decanter.

When they reached the historic Germantown mansion, a middle-aged woman who introduced herself as "Jan, Mrs. Fortley's assistant" answered the door. She made apologies on behalf of Mrs. Fortley. "We were unsuccessful in reaching you this morning to alert you to the change of venue." Francine and Ursula looked at each other, then back at the assistant. They explained that they were in church and had not checked their phones.

Jan continued, "Mrs. Fortely is a touch under the weather and asked that you please meet her, instead, at this address?" She extended an old-fashioned calling card with a residential address in the upscale Chestnut Hill ZIP code.

"Shall I call her to expect you momentarily?"

"Yes, of course. We'll head right over," Francine responded.

Jan gave a look that said, *good answer.*

"Very well. I will let her know you are on the way."

Neither of them uttered a word until they were safely in the car as if Jan would be able to read their lips from the distance of the door, window, or wherever she was. They knew it didn't make sense to behave that way, but for some reason, it felt like the thing to do.

"This here, this doesn't make any damned sense!" Ursula said as she started the car. They both checked their phones. No messages. Francine burst into laughter.

"She's crazy! I love her already. She's running us and doesn't even care to be sly about it," Francine shook her head and laughed as she tapped the address into her GPS.

Ursula was not amused. "She has an hour and a half and we're out of there. And she better be good and lame when we get there," she chuckled. "This is your neck of the woods. Do you know where we're going?"

"I have an idea. It's pretty much down the street. Make a U-turn," Francine said kicking of her pumps to rub her feet together and clicking on the passenger seat heat.

After driving a mile or so down Germantown Avenue, they pulled into the private driveway and drove down about a quarter-mile to a huge stone estate. They parked the car at the end of the driveway almost in front of the door.

"Who would have known all this was back up in here! I guess this is where she *actually* lives," Ursula said, insulted that she was first received at the public residence.

"Hey, you can't be too careful. I'm sure she's seen her share of predators in all forms. Don't take it personally, *Miz* St. James!"

"Oh, shut up!"

"Pull yourself together!" Francine said in a hush as they rang the doorbell. "She is our Hibiscus Suite benefactor."

"True. True," Ursula said composing herself.

The door opened in an instant. They both were visibly taken aback.

"Oh, I didn't mean to startle you. I was just coming to the door to see if the gate opened. I've had trouble with it lately. Come in, come in," the elderly Mrs. Fortley stepped back ushering them into the foyer. She was wearing ornate slippers and a gold silk floor-length vintage dressing gown. Her striking silver hair was curled up neatly at her ears. Her smooth skin defied her age. The gold gown, which she wore fastened up to the neck, was flattering against her maple complexion.

"It's delightful to see you again, Mrs. Fortley." Ursula leaned in to greet her with a cheek-to-cheek hug.

"Mrs. Isola Fortley, allow me to present Dr. Francine Marie Carty." Appreciating Ursula's formality, Mrs. Fortley offered Francine a warm smile.

"It is a pleasure to make your acquaintance, Mrs. Fortley. Thank you for inviting us to your lovely estate," Francine greeted her with deference, fighting the urge to curtsey.

"Thank you for accepting the invitation," she appraised Francine approvingly. "I'll take your coats," she said clearing a rattle in her throat. "Please do excuse me! I have a tickle in my throat I can't seem to shake. I sent Jan to the other place, so it's just us."

Francine used the opportunity to offer the strong tea. "Tis the season for such nuisances. I brought you a little something that might just do the trick," she said handing Mrs. Fortley the tall narrow black gift bag with her family's name and insignia printed discretely in steel grey script.

"Thank you, my dear. I'll see that it does." Mrs. Fortley accepted the bag as if she were expecting it and tucked it under her arm. "Would you like me to put those in water, Ursula?" Ursula was so enthralled by the show Francine was putting on with Mrs. Fortley, she had forgotten the flowers.

"Please. Enjoy."

With Francine's coat and the Carty bag on one arm, it was the first time Francine noticed her coat was the exact same hue as the family insignia. Winnie was relentless but apparently knew what she was doing. Mrs. Fortley adjusted the load so that the coat and bag were in one arm as an ensemble with Ursula's coat and flowers in the other—unevenly as if she were an imbalanced scale. The image was peculiar.

"Let us help you with that, Mrs. Fortley!" They both began to follow her.

"No, no. You girls make yourselves comfortable in the salon. It's to your left. We're set up there. I'll be right with you and won't keep you long." Mrs. Fortley glided off in the opposite direction.

The salon was an unexpected but stylish juxtaposition of modernity and traditional décor. The converted remote-operated fireplace roared from behind glass doors through a mother of pearl, tiled fireplace. Pastel oriental rugs covered huge spaces of the bamboo flooring, and the seating consisted of modern designer originals: over-sized settees, chaises, and twin tufted sofas on each side of the table where the tea was set. The grandfather clock in the foyer struck half past 4 when Mrs. Fortley strode into the salon carrying a tray with three plates, cake forks, and a banana cream pie and spatula. Francine and Ursula moaned in unison.

"Ladies, today, we indulge," she insisted they have the pie with the tea.

They talked shop, family, Philadelphia, and friendship. Mrs. Fortley was pleased to confirm that Ursula and Francine had become friends and were dining regularly at the Hibiscus Suite. They toasted to friendship.

"Francine, shall we have a taste of your family beverage?" Mrs. Fortley suggested.

"Certainly," Francine agreed. "Allow me." She poured an ounce into each teacup and added two parts tea.

"Oh, yes," Mrs. Fortley said after the first sip. "This should do nicely. My throat will be clear in no time."

Disengaging with each passing minute, Ursula had several cups of tea while Mrs. Fortley got to know Francine, also over several cups. Francine knew how her potion worked, so she stopped after the first ounce and drank just tea after that. When Ursula made her second wobbly trip to the powder room, Mrs. Fortley watched her intently, until the door closed firmly. Then she turned to Francine, resting her teacup gently and soberly on its saucer.

"Listen to me, Miss Carty. Quick. I asked you here to tell you something. You have an important opportunity ahead of you tomorrow. The Search is a once-in-a-lifetime invitation, and I want you to get it. Roseline has endorsed you, and that means a lot to me. She likes you and says you're what we need. So here's what, rather *who* you need to know. My proxy is Mrs. Emma Johnson. She is also my niece. Not a word will pass her lips outside of her introduction. Her job is to be my eyes and ears, not my mouth. The other person, I understand, could be a problem for you: Mrs. Stephanie Lashley."

Francine's eyes widened.

"We do our homework, my dear. She's definitely sizing you up, seeing as though you stole the heart of the young man her Patrice had hers set on. Don't worry. You did that *fiiiine* young man a favor and Stephanie, too. They would have made a miserable family. It's just that now that you are the candidate, she's reevaluating her decision to shut him out of their lives. But you don't need to worry about Stephanie. She puts on a strong front, but Roseline runs the show. She's the one who needs to see a demonstration of grace and unwavering strength on your part. Stephanie, poor thing, is still running from her past. Her family fell on hard times, and it was the generosity of friends and *extended ... relations* ...that sustained them until her marriage to Mr. Lashley restored their status and wealth. She is absolutely consumed with keeping that brief but devastating chapter discrete and, of course, insuring that they are never in that position again. Just keep that in mind tomorrow. It's important to know where people are coming from. Understand their fears, you see. But know this: If you present her an opportunity, she will strike."

Francine sat with her mouth ajar. She couldn't believe Mrs. Fortley was alluding to the secret of princess trophy's scandalous paternity less than 24 hours after she herself learned of it. It was stunning. In her family's line of work, the entire family had plenty of practice with discretion. Discretion was one of the cornerstones of their success. Because people tended to reveal all kinds of information when they are grieving, those with the most delicate situations buried with Cartys. They could be counted on to "bury the dead" in every sense of the term.

The sound of the powder room door opening snapped Francine out of her thoughts, and she abruptly shut her lips, embarrassed and reeling from all that Mrs. Fortley had said.

"Dear Ursula, are you all right?" Mrs. Fortley shifted gears, fawning over Ursula. "I'm afraid I've kept you girls too long and corrupted you with the drink," she laughed. "Francine, it looks as if you'll be doing the driving this evening. I'll get your things."

Francine took Ursula's keys as Ms. Fortley left the room to get the ladies' coats. "Somebody had a good time."

"Why did you let me drink your *burial brew*!?" Ursula slurred.

"Nobody told you to have four cups of tea!"

"Five!" Ursula barked. "And I want to know everything that bird said while I was in the bathroom. She ain't *slick*!"

"*Quiet!* I'll fill you in later. Right now, I need to get you straightened up. I have something for that, too. But you'll have to stay at my place tonight, okay?"

"Whatever," Ursula sat down in the chair and crossed her ankles to model composure as Mrs. Fortley returned with their coats.

"Keep the windows cracked some. The cool air will help," Mrs. Fortley advised, sober as a judge and sounding better.

"Yes, ma'am," Francine said as she tied the belt on her coat and helped Ursula on with hers.

"Thank you for having us, Mrs. Fortley. It's been a pleasure," Ursula managed.

"I do apologize dear. I should have guessed it runs in the family. Fleurette was a terrible drinker!" Mrs. Fortley consoled Ursula. "Too much of a lady, I suppose."

Ursula nodded, "Oh, yes. Grandmother was an impeccable lady," she changed direction shaking her head no.

What a display. Francine would relish the memory.

"It was lovely to meet you, Mrs. Fortley. Your hospitality won't soon be forgotten," Francine grasped her hand in both of hers. "Thank you," she whispered in her ear as she hugged her goodbye.

"Knock 'em dead," Mrs. Fortley whispered in return.

Mrs. Fortley stood on the step in her dressing gown watching the friends closely as Francine helped Ursula into the passenger seat, buckled her in, and drove up the long drive onto the main road.

"We're going to be just fine," Mrs. Fortley said to herself as she retreated into the house and closed the door.

***

The next morning, as she sent Ursula on her way with an antidote to the burial brew, Francine did her best to follow her Monday routine. She popped in to see Roseline, but Noah said she would not be in the office at all that day. Just as well—business as usual. Her students were happy to be done with midterms and didn't have too many questions regarding the midterm grades she posted. With a little extra time to spare, Francine arrived at the bar a little early for her shift. Earl, the bartender who worked days, was happy to see her.

"Hello, Lady! You're here early today," he greeted her in an upbeat voice. Philadelphia had a long history of being receptive of the gay and lesbian community. Earl lived in the "gayborhood" section of city with his partner, while pursuing his MBA part time. He was tall, dark-haired with striking green eyes. He was also an extraordinary bartender/mixologist, and being eye candy didn't hurt.

"How's tricks today, beautiful?" Francine gave Earl a warm greeting.

"You're about to find out, Wonderbra! There's a political convention in town," he said, flashing a thick wad of cash tips.

"Ooooh goody!" Francine cracked her knuckles and pretended to adjust the twins. She and Earl had an ongoing debate on whether customers responded better to bartenders with features they found attractive. She teased him about his hair and eyes, he teased about her perky C cups.

Earl slung his bag over his head and across his body. "Gotta dash, professor. Class presentation tonight," he said as he exited the bar to the lobby.

"Knock 'em dead!" she yelled behind him.

Earl was right. The bar was a constant stream of tabs and tips in suits for the following two hours, before thinning out to a few of the regulars. Francine had already made enough in tips to go home with plenty of spending cash and extra for a good grocery run to Whole Foods. With an hour remaining in her shift, one of her regulars greeted her.

Byron Sellers was a C-level executive at a major telecommunications conglomerate with headquarters around the corner from the Four Seasons. He stopped in just about daily to wait out the rush hour traffic or to entertain other executives over drinks. He was a great conversationalist but seemed to carry heavy baggage that the drinks couldn't buoy.

"You must be having a good night, with all of these big wigs in town?" he said.

"Mama's bringing home a roast tonight!" she laughed.

He joined her. "Hey, hey! The taxpayers dollars are being well spent."

"And I do thank them all," she patted the bulging apron that held her tips. "The usual, Mr. Sellers?"

"Please," he slapped his black card on the bar and slid it toward Francine to start his tab.

They exchanged the usual small talk, and Francine shared that she was going home tomorrow evening for a long weekend. She gave him the short, casual version of the weekend's events.

"So what's this big thing you have tomorrow?" he asked. "Isn't the Sherman an electronic submission?"

Francine clarified that she had already pressed send on the Sherman application, and that it was this "conversation" she had tomorrow that was freaking her out.

"Conversation," he repeated mysteriously.

At that moment, it struck Francine that he might actually have heard of the secret grant, being that he was "Bobby Billionaire" and all.

"Sounds like some Namaste, one love, we are the world lingo my ex was into. An argument was never an argument with her; a lie never a lie. Everything was a *conversation*. Oh, except the divorce. She was crystal clear about that," he paused to take a gulp of his drink. "Eh, she was right, though. And you know what?"

"What?" Francine had learned the importance of listening.

"She didn't fight me for a dime. She was such a lady about the whole thing. I wrote her a blank check. She wrote it out as matching funds to a foundation she started with some friends when she sued the crap out of her boss the same year. The craft—oh no, that's the witchy shit. The Firm, maybe?"

It couldn't be.

Francine almost leapt over the bar, grabbing Byron's immaculately manicured, hairy hand, "The Search?!" she shrieked.

"*That's* it!" Byron turned up his glass with his free hand, "You know it?"

"Byron! The "conversation" I have tomorrow is for *The Search* Fellowship. What can you tell me about it?!"

"Nothing," he said over a cube of ice in his mouth. "I haven't heard a word about it since she deposited the check."

Francine realized she missed a beat, "Wait! *You were married to Roseline Mercer*?"

"Yes. *I* was. Roseline Mercer Sellers Mercer," he raised his glass toasting Roseline in absentia.

"Well, I'll be damned," Francine stared at Byron incredulously.

"What? You can't believe a woman like Rose would be married to me?" he said, laughing.

"No. Well, that *is* interesting to imagine," she chided him playfully. "I just can't believe the coincidence. The world is way too small."

"Yeah, well, we were young and in love a very long time ago. Met in a hostel in Tunisia. Those were good times while they lasted. We traveled most of the world together and damn near the entire U.S. Then, we came home. When we did, the honeymoon was over—fast!" He paused and took a small sip of the generous double shot refill Francine poured him.

"You tell her I said hello and that you get my vote! *O crème sempre sobe ao topo …*"

"Yes, *the cream always rises to the top*. Someone recently said that to me, but I can't remember who. Did you learn Portuguese in your travels with the former Mrs. Sellers?" Francine asked.

"Yeah," he finished the double shot.

Geesh, he can sure put it away, Francine thought.

"We ended up in Brazil, but we met at the Santa Monica hostel. Even as a hosteller, she insisted on the best: HI-USA all the way, not the grungy ones you see in the movies. She had me convinced she was Brazilian, teaching me Portuguese phrases for hours from the top bunk. I was willing to learn anything. Truthfully? I was drawn to her like a magnet. It wasn't until the heat of the moment she started speaking English. Had me fooled. Said she wanted to see who I was when I thought she didn't know what I was saying. Those were good times."

"Go 'head Byron! Had Dean Mercer speaking in *bilingual* tongues!?" Francine teased.

They clinked glasses and laughed.

"Sounds like you've spoken that language yourself," Byron chided.

"Yessss, thank you Lawd! But, we are talking about *you*," Francine faked shaking off chills.

"This whole thing is so interesting. I was actually thinking of doing the Fellowship in Brazil if I get it, but now I'm considering a place I've never been. I feel like I a need a BIG change," Francine said, redirecting the conversation.

"If you've hitched your wagon to Roseline … that is precisely what you are in for, young lady," he said, now standing next to his chair.

"Looks like your shift is over," he said, nodding a greeting to her relief bartender. He signed for his tab and slipped her a $50 tip.

"Thank you, Bryon."

"I'll call for your car while you clock out," he gestured for her valet ticket.

"I love a gentleman!" she said as she transferred the cash from her apron to her purse under the bar and threw the apron in with the used towels.

"Watch yourself, now. If I were 30 years younger, you'd be in trouble!" Byron said as he slipped his credit card into his shirt pocket.

Francine gave him her complimentary employee parking pass, and he headed to the lobby.

She exchanged formalities of the shift change with the closing bartender and made her way to the valet stand just outside. Byron was already in the wind, his suit jacket flapping as he jogged across the street to the skyscraper that bore the name of his company. Francine thought about twentysomething Roseline and Byron traveling around the world staying in hostels, idealistic and in love. Neither had remarried. He'd never even mentioned an actual reason why they broke up. She wondered if Roseline still loved Byron at all. It was clear that he still loved her.

"Here's your car," the valet hopped out and held her car door. "Mr. Sellers has already taken care of the tip." All of the service staff seemed to know and appreciate Byron as a generous regular who treated them well. Francine counted herself among them.

***

When Francine arrived at her place, she parked outside and just sat in the car. Her apartment was actually a small quaint carriage house turned guesthouse, on the border of the historic Germantown and bucolic West Mount Airy neighborhoods. It had been renovated by the family who owned the larger house on the property. Her landlord explained that the rent was how he and his wife hoped to pay off the renovation. Francine moved there the previous year after two years in a traditional apartment building, a lifestyle that no longer appealed to her. The guesthouse was very comfortable, and the rent was the right price. The family respected her privacy and were very responsive to seldom-needed repairs.

However, when Francine's mother first saw it, she exclaimed, in horror, that it looked like her baby girl was living in slave quarters behind the big house.

Slave quarters, be damned! For Francine, it beat paying double the rent for a beige box with God-knows-who for neighbors and incognito landlords. Plus, Francine could keep a small herb garden to grow her own basil and mint. The Hansons were delightful people, and the arrangement was a win-win. That said, Francine still hated the idea of paying rent—paying someone else's mortgage—instead of owning her own place.

She collected her things and trudged the 10 steps to the front door. Until that very moment, Francine had not realized how exhausted she was from the whirlwind of the past several weeks. She decided to go straight to bed. No bath, no shower. Due to an inexplicable fixation she'd had forever, she *would* wash her feet, though.

The next morning, Francine barely remembered arriving home.

I must have been on autopilot, she thought. For the first time in weeks, she felt rested. The day had finally come. It was time for the "conversation." Francine took a long, hot shower and enjoyed a decidedly leisurely morning preparing for her day. Revisiting the Bennie and Winnie section of her closet, she selected a tailored black pantsuit with pale grey pinstripes and steel blue silk blouse that Ursula suggested. Her accessories would be a double strand pearl bracelet and pearl earrings. She slipped on her loafers but threw a pair of black Mary-Jane t-strap spectator pumps in her hobo bag, which reminded her to put her good purse in the trunk. Initially, she planned to get changed in Ursula's office, since adjuncts shared a common space. Instead, she decided to get comfortable in what she'd be wearing during the conversation. Dressing at home also reduced the risk of forgetting an important item of clothing or accessory. Frankly, Francine was tired of worrying about it and was ready for the entire ordeal to be over and done with. She was regretting having whipped up such a fuss with everyone.

The day proceeded uneventfully until she entered the dean's office at 3:55 p.m. Noah was waiting for her.

"Afternoon, Dr. Carty." His eyes shone with excitement.

"Hello, Noah. I guess this is it!"

"Dr. Mercer has asked me to walk you over to the executive conference room. You all will have more privacy there. This way."

His formality made her nervous. She walked with him down the hall and into an addition to the building that she'd never visited. They stopped at a corner office. "Here we are," Noah said in a lowered voice. He gave a light knock and opened the door, then retreated. Assembled around a formal tea setting were three women: Roseline, who stood to welcome and formally introduce Francine who was seated at the head of the table. Mrs. Fortley's proxy gave a polite nod but a firm handshake. Mrs. Lashley met Francine with cool eyes and a limp fingertip-only handshake. All of the ladies were dressed in dark pantsuits and power blouses and assessed Francine from head to toe as she took her seat: Roseline, with encouragement. The proxy, with approval. And Mrs. Lashley, with a trace of impressed regret.

God bless you, Isola Fortley, Francine thought. She would rock this meeting on Mrs. Fortley's behalf as well as her own.

The conversation proceeded exactly as Mrs. Fortley said it would. Francine and Roseline conversed, rehashing the same questions from their meetings only in a more formal tone for their audience. The two spectators watched intently and reviewed the written materials of Francine's application over designer bifocal half-frames. Francine channeled her mother's teachings, her two years of Jack and Jill, and Mrs. Fortley's warnings to offer an expert presentation of competence, composure, and grace. One hour and fifteen minutes later, Roseline was escorting her from the room after a repeat of the two confident and one non-committed handshakes.

Francine couldn't help but to notice that it was the longest time she had seen Roseline interact *without* actually drinking tea. The settings sat untouched, as if for decoration. As a result, her voice seemed to be growing more dry and coarse by the sentence. There was something familiar about the way her tone modulated—a distinct cadence that resonated with Francine, though she didn't know why. Standing on opposite sides of the threshold, Roseline thanked Francine for her time.

"Exceptional conversation, Dr. Carty," she croaked.

"You've prepared well. I'll inform you of the committee's decision two weeks from today."

Francine smiled at the compliment.

With a wink and a whisper, the timbre of Roseline's voice turned again to something strangely familiar her.

"*O crème sempe sobe ao topo* ... Zora."

7

Francine had two options. She could take her meds before she boarded the plane to VA in order to avoid the fibro pain that would inevitably come from the stress of traveling or forgo her meds and be able to enjoy a glass of wine and a delicious book without all the side effects that were bound to make her loopy well before she landed.

"Well that's a no-brainer," she said out loud as she threw her meds and a small bag of toiletries into her overnight case. She stopped to rub her hand along the smooth tattered leather of the case and was assaulted by memories of two Christmases prior when Garrison presented the designer bag to her filled with sexy lingerie he'd picked out.

"For all the wonderful overnight rendezvous we'll take together," he'd said.

Francine chuckled. *Yeah okay, Sir.*

In that moment, she couldn't bring herself to consider the lull that had formed in their relationship at the moment. So much had happened. Her heart and mind were still reeling with the revelation that Roseline was Chase. *How was that even possible?*

This changed everything, in her mind.

What do I do?

Francine sat on the edge of the bed, staring at the wall she'd painted red on a whim a year ago despite the fact that it violated her lease. Even though her landlords were cool, she still got? pleasure in these kinds of tiny rebellions. But this situation was far from small.

She hated having things held over her head or used as weapons against her, and she wondered if that's how this would pan out. She also wondered if she'd garnered the favor of the committee based on her own merit or the influence of Roseline/Chase.

Francine shook out of her head the images of herself on the phone saying those things, doing those things, to the voice she'd just learned belonged to her dean. She wouldn't make it to the airport if she allowed herself to break down. She needed to mentally table her inner dialogue until she could get home and talk to the one person who could help her make sense of it all.

The timing of her doorbell was perfect. It was the cab driver.

***

"ROOOOOBBBBBBBIII!!"

Francine ran around to the other side of the baggage claim carousel and scooped up the petite woman dressed in Peace Corps sweats. When she spun her around, the woman shouted, "Girl if you don't put me down!" but the grin on her face said that she enjoyed every minute of it. Francine was what Robena called her big, little sister. The free spirit of their family with a heart as wide as an ocean. She loved every bit of her crazy.

"Frankie!"

Francine put her sister down but continued to embrace her.

"Robbi."

Robena stared at her baby sister. She then put both hands on her face and brought Frankie nose to nose with her. It was something she'd been doing since they were little kids. It was her way of letting Francine know that she could "see" her. Really *see* her.

"Uh huh. That's what I thought. What's wrong?"

Francine closed her eyes to stop the tears from falling.

"Your spirit ain't right chile'," Robena said with the manufactured accent they'd use whenever they'd secretly mock the elder members of their family who lived most of their lives in Montserrat before the volcano eruptions in the '90s.

Francine chuckled and moved Robena's hands. She'd expected that her sister's radar would be in tip-top shape. Grabbing her overnight bag and laptop case, she nodded toward the sliding doors.

"Let's go get a drink," Francine finally said as she grabbed her sister's arm to walk out the doors.

Robbi stopped quickly. "Drink? Didn't you take your meds before you left?"

Francine sighed and rolled her eyes in a slight fit of irritation. It seemed like everyone wanted to police her health.

"No, no, no. Not yet. I needed a drink so I'm waiting."

Robena looked skeptical. It wasn't that she was uptight. In fact, most of what little Frankie learned about life, including boys and later men, was firmly guided by the conversations she heard and overheard about her sister's exploits. But Robena had been working for the government and her perspective had changed quite a bit. She'd seen too much loss and pain. Plus, her standards were much higher when it came to her baby sister.

"And it seems like *you* need to loosen up, too," Francine said as she bumped her sister's narrow hip with her own.

"Loosen that up, gyal!"

The two sisters both laughed loudly, startling the people waiting for their bags next them.

But they couldn't care less. Frankie and Robbi walked out of the airport together arm in arm.

***

The Rocks.

It had been years since Francine had visited the place where she once found so much peace. This is why she loved her sister so much. She knew exactly where to take her. Yes, they'd stopped off at Obsidian for a couple of drinks and Robena caught Francine up on all her adventures overseas. In fact, when she'd shared with her more information on her upcoming trip to Botswana, Francine's heart leaped a bit. Not with envy but with admiration. Francine wanted that same sense of purpose and the willingness to go all out for it.

She wanted to be able to do work that mattered on a much larger scale. She loved her work in the classroom. It was a chance to influence the minds of the next generation of scholars. But it was with her research that she felt she could make a greater impact. She firmly believed that once you studied a culture, its language, and social customs, in particular, and were able to translate the nuances of that culture to a wider audience, you become instrumental in elevating that culture in the eyes of the mainstream, not for the culture's sake but for the sake of a world who desperately needs to find meaning and identification in all of humanity. Maybe break this up into two sentences? It's a little long as is.

Francine knew the opportunities that she had in front of her would allow her to do exactly that. There was only one dean-sized obstacle to overcome.

Francine and Robena sat in silence for a while watching the river kiss the shoreline. Not much had changed in over two decades. In fact, the sisters, lost in their individual memories, were both certain that if they'd gotten out of the car and walked over to the lone tree that drank from the shore and spread its branches wide above the water, they'd still see their names carved into its bark from years ago.

But they didn't get out. They talked. Robena broke the ice.

"So what's going on with you?" she said.

The alcohol loosened Francine's tongue a bit as she shared with her sister what happened during the meeting with the committee and finally, Roseline's sly reveal.

Robena sat and listened. She wore a well-practiced stoic face that not even Francine could gauge. Nevertheless, Francine knew that her sister didn't judge her. She was probably the only person on the planet who didn't. After Francine exhausted herself sharing how she felt about the situation, all the back and forth she'd gone through since leaving Roseline's office that day, she breathed deeply. But instead of releasing a breath in her exhale, what came out was a sob that even she didn't expect. It came from deep down in the pit of her stomach.

Her initial thought was that she regretted not taking her meds. Most of the pills had an antidepressant component that would have held back such a display of her vulnerability. But she was sure time travel wasn't an option.

Robena picked up Francine's left hand, held it between both of her own, and stroked it gently as her baby sister cried. Then as Francine's tears began to wane, Robena patted the hand that she held and laid it back in her sister's lap.

"Listen, Frankie. You've always been the one."

Francine's bowed head popped up and turned toward Robena in protest. Robena raised her hand to stop her.

"You have the biggest heart of anyone I've ever known. I get why this bothers you. You not only feel like something you did, a private decision you made, has been exposed, but that you have also exposed someone else. Someone who has great power over you but is just as broken as any of us."

Francine closed her eyes and allowed her sister's accuracy to reach her.

"But now," Robena continued, "I need you to shift from how you *feel* about this to how you *think* about it. I need you to be strategic."

Francine opened her eyes as Robena went on. "When I say you are the one, I mean, you are the one who will elevate the Carty name, as dad used to say."

Hearing this was so bizarre for Francine. In her mind, Robena was always the "the one." She was the one who volunteered at homeless shelters while still in high school. She was the one who spent all of her adult life serving others.

Robena raised her hand again. "I know what you're thinking. But what you don't realize, what you've never realized, is that there is an enormous gift in you that must get to the world. So you need to look at this scenario strategically and ask yourself what option is going to best allow you to share that gift with the world. Don't allow your frustrations or emotions or fear to allow you to deviate from what you know you must do. This thing with these women is an excellent opportunity. You need to do everything to protect that."

Francine considered what Robena was saying. It all resonated with her. "But how am I going to look at Dean …"

Robena threw her hands up in semi-fake exasperation. "SO WHAT? The woman was lonely and called a sex line! Yes, pretending to be a man … which I'll admit is a little freaky … but big deal! That kind of stuff happens more than you think," Robena winked at her baby sister.

Francine's mouth flew open. "Whaaaaaaaat?! Not you, Robena Corrine Carty!"

Robena looked at Francine from the corner of her eyes. "What? I didn't say anything?!"

The sisters laughed in their loud way again, and Francine felt 100% better. Robena, satisfied that her baby girl was going to be okay, changed the subject.

"So, for either fellowship, where are you thinking about doing your research?" she asked.

"Well, I was initially thinking about Brazil, but since talking to you, West Africa has also been on my mind."

"West Africa it is then."

"Wait, wait, wait..." Francine waved her hands. "I haven't made a decision yet. Why not Brazil?"

Robena smiled. "If you are in Brazil, then how am I going to keep an eye on you?"

Francine laughed. "Oh, so that's why you want me to go to Africa!"

"Listen, Botswana is almost 3,000 miles south of West Africa, so obviously, I'm not going to be swooping in for weekend pajama parties. But hey, we'll be on the same continent, and if I do need to get to you, it would be a whole lot easier. Plus, you've been talking about studying in Ghana for years, why not do it now?"

Once again, Francine's big sister had given her some wise counsel.

"Yeah, you're right. I mean, I did my whole dissertation on the national presentations of Kwame Nkrumah's legacy there. It would be great to learn the colloquial presentations as well …"

"See! There you go. It sure sounds like you need to be in West Africa to me!"

Francine chuckled. "Alright, alright. I'll think about it."

"You do that," Robena said. "And remember, whatever you decide, be strategic."

"Strategic. Got it."

***

Francine returned to Philadelphia refreshed. She dove headfirst into her work, making sure that she was prepared for whatever decision was made. Per her sister's advice, she wrote down her strategy, including a very detailed five-year plan. She also avoided Garrison. He'd called her multiple times since she'd been back but, for a reason she couldn't put her finger on, she couldn't bring herself to talk to him. She'd even avoided the cafeteria where they'd usually meet for lunch. She held her student consults in Ursula's office instead of the adjunct room. She just needed her mind clear for the following weeks and his presence very much clouded everything. She knew what Garrison wanted from her. He wanted tradition: the picket fence, the yearly trips to Disney with the 2.5 kids, and summers at some society resort beachfront. She found his traditions restrictive and preferred a less inhibitive lifestyle.

But Garrison was nothing but persistent. He wasn't going to let her just fade to black in his life, especially not since she'd become connected in all the ways that he needed her to be. Francine was slowly becoming a part of an inner circle that he'd never been able to be a part of completely, even when he was practically married to it.

***

One night Francine finally decided to take a break from all her preparations. She'd had some pretty intense fibro flares over the previous couple of days, and she knew that the pains were signs that she needed to slow down and rest. Yes, she knew it was good to be in stealth mode when it came to her plans, her next moves, but she also knew, at least intellectually, that none of it mattered if she wasn't healthy. Her plan that night was to take a nice, hot steamy shower, spend some extra time tending to her toes and nails, re-twist her hair that was growing like crazy into a fluffy halo, and curl up in her bed with her Oreo cookies to watch some mind-numbing and terribly salacious reality show.

When she stepped out of the shower, Francine heard a rather urgent knock at the door. The person must have been knocking for some time because by the time she heard it, it sounded like the police about to make a bust. Francine was concerned because it was way too late for anyone unexpected to be showing up at her house. She picked up the taser Robbi had given her a few years back, engaged it, and walked slowly over to the door.

"Who is it?"

The voice was steady, even calm. It totally didn't match the insistence of the knock.

"The man you've been avoiding."

She recognized it like it was her own.

"Garrison. Not tonight."

This time agitation rose in his voice. "Oh, so you're actually going to talk to me through the door, sending me on my way like I'm a Jehovah's Witness or a Girl Scout?"

Francine smiled a little. He really did have a way with words. Garrison had no idea how close his little metaphor really hit. He was very much like those Oreos on her bed. He was *just* like those crack-laced Thin Mints sold by those pint-sized hustlers outside the grocery. You can't eat one bite. You can't wean yourself off of them. You have to go cold turkey. But a part of Francine knew she wasn't being fair. She needed to have the conversation with him.

"Give me a second."

Francine slipped off her head wrap, ran some cocoa butter across her lips, and slipped on her robe. As soon as she opened the door, she knew that she'd made a mistake. Garrison stood there like a bronze statue, chiseled in all the right places. Under his classic wool pea coat, he wore a white shirt that shone brighter against the brown of his skin. She thought he glowed. Like an angel or a devil or both, she wasn't quite sure yet. The top two buttons of his shirt were unbuttoned, and she could see the curly, jet-black hair on his chest. His jeans were ironed within an inch of their life, the crease sharp as a knife. He was so country—and she loved it. His goatee, which he'd begun growing before she left, was filling in nicely. And his eyes were … well, he was Garrison. His eyes bored into her, searching her.

"I haven't heard from you. How was your trip?" he asked.

Then, his eyes brazenly wandered up and down the contours of her body, lingering at his favorite places.

Francine could feel the beads of sweat forming under her arms, under her breasts, and between her thighs. In an effort to cool things down, she backed away and opened the door, silently inviting him in.

"So?" he said as he stood next to the small breakfast counter.

"So what, Garrison?" Francine avoided his eyes and busied herself with random items on the counter.

"Why haven't I heard from you?" he searched her eyes.

She couldn't respond. She didn't want her voice to betray her. The moment was thick with intensity. The synapses in her brain were firing all kinds of mixed messages. *Caution. Green light. Stop. Go. Warning. Touch him. Don't you dare!*

A part of her was angry with herself because she could tell by the smirk on his face he knew exactly the effect he was having on her. He was milking it, reeling her in minute by minute. She felt manipulated and out of control.

Garrison took a step toward her. She took a step back. He grinned. She didn't. He took another step toward her. She took another step back. This second time he tilted his head, slightly perplexed. He'd certainly expected some resistance but not this much. *Why are you fighting me,* he thought. The sexual tension he felt between them was undeniable, and he didn't understand why all of sudden she was trying to quench what was an obvious thirst. He didn't want to have to convince her. That felt all kinds of wrong. He needed to give her an out. This was one of those moments when his brother's words rang true: "Man, you are more of a feminist than some chicks I know." He wasn't sure about that, but he did want the woman he was with to be totally and completely sold on the encounter.

"Would you like for me to leave?" his voice was just above a whisper.

Yes, it was a bit passive aggressive, but it was all he had in the moment. He didn't want to leave. He wanted to kiss her. He wanted to touch her, taste her, and hold her.

Smart move, Francine thought to herself. This had become a chess match. He'd made a move that had exposed him, one that had the greatest risk, but depending on her move, it could have the greatest reward. The one thing she'd promised herself when she'd returned from Maryland was that she would stand completely and fully in her truth, no matter what that looked like or how hard that was. Her truth was sometimes ugly and sometimes even worked against her best interest. But it was hers.

Francine walked over to Garrison and placed her hand inside his open shirt. He reached up and wrapped his strong hands around her wrist. He lifted her hand to his face and began kissing each of her fingers, then nuzzled his face in her palm. His lips then traveled the inside of her wrist to her forearm. Francine closed her eyes and let the tears fall on the inside.

***

The alarm awakened Francine the next morning at 6 a.m. She had six more weeks of what she begun calling the dark 30 class— 8 a.m. It was the class that none of the full-time and tenured professors wanted but every adjunct trying to make themselves look like a "team player" in hopes of getting hired full time fought to get. Garrison, of course, didn't have that issue.

"Wake up, Garrison. I have class. Don't you have a lab this morning?"

He grumbled something unintelligible to himself and turned on his side.

Francine sighed and tried again. This time she threw one of the decorative pillows that, as usual, found itself strewn across the floor after their night of love. She tossed it gently at this head.

"Yo, G!" she grinned as she called him by the rapper name he'd christened himself during one of their failed attempts at role-play. "Get up, maaaan!"

Garrison grumbled again and said in his raspy morning voice, "Alright, alright, Patrice. In a minute."

Francine was stunned. Rage filled her as she jumped on the bed and pushed him off the side of it with all her strength.

"What?! What did you just say?! Patrice? Really?!"

"Owww!" Garrison screamed grabbing his elbow that had slammed into the bookcase next to his side of the bed.

Francine fought back the tears as Garrison quickly picked himself off the floor. His face was confused at first and then mortified as he recalled what had just happened.

"No, Frankie. No, no. I didn't mean …"

Francine began picking up all of Garrison's clothes on the floor and stuffing them in a plastic grocery bag that had been sitting on the counter.

"You're sleeping with her, aren't you?! What? I go away for a few days and you go screw your ex?"

Garrison ran over to Francine who picked up the Taser that still sat on the counter from the night before. She pointed it at him. "Don't come near me."

"No, Frankie. I'm not sleeping with her, I promise." Garrison's voice had reached an anxious pitch. He couldn't believe how stupid he was in that moment.

Francine became frustrated with the bag she was holding, the bag she was trying to fill with anything in her house that belonged to the man in front of her, but in a fit of anger, she just threw it onto the floor. Finally, something broke inside her. Sliding to her knees on the kitchen floor she cried. *I knew I shouldn't have let you in. I shouldn't have let you in.*

Garrison kneeled down beside her. Francine looked up, and he noticed that the anger that filled her eyes a second before was gone. Sadness like he'd never seen before had taken its place.

"Have you seen her?" she asked quietly.

"No." He paused and then corrected himself.

"I mean, yes, but ..."

The anger returned and Francine pushed Garrison who was still kneeling in front of her. She threw him off balance so much that he ended up seated on the floor.

"Okay, she called me. I had to go to NJIT in Newark and ..." Garrison was hesitant to share the next part.

"And?" Francine stared back at him.

"And we met for lunch in the city."

"Awfully convenient since I was gone."

Garrison dropped his head into his hands. "It was not planned. It just happened that way. She'd lost someone close to her and ... I don't know ... I thought I could help."

Francine laughed. She laughed long and hard. Garrison watched her, and for the first time, she saw a glimmer of fear in his eyes.

"What so funny?" he said quietly.

"Yeah she lost someone, alright. Her God-daddy slash Daddy." Francine laughed again even as the tears poured from her eyes.

Garrison shook his head. "What? You're not making any sense."

Francine wiped her face and stood up. For what felt like forever, she just stood there silent.

Garrison awkwardly picked his six-foot-two frame off the small kitchen's tile floor. His boxers clung to his strong thighs and his chest heaved. He reached out to Francine, but she held up her hand as she'd seen her sister do many, many times before.

"Just go. Don't you have to be at the lab?"

Her voice was vacant. It was resolute. She didn't want to care anymore. She was choosing to detach. For her own sake and his.

8

Garrison auto-piloted home in a haze of regret. Was he actually the cliché that just played out in that scene? It was as if he'd had an out-of-body experience that he tried to make sense of over the next several hours. In the same manner he drove home, Garrison climbed the stairs to his apartment on the third floor of the huge Victorian row house. As he passed his beloved old-school entertainment center, he pressed play. The custom compilations served as the soundtrack to his life—anything was better than the battle going on in his head at the moment. Fully disrobed by the time he made it to the bathroom at the end of the long hallway, Garrison avoided the mirror and stepped into the shower. He bowed to let the steaming water pelt his crown, cascading around to his face until it ran off of the tips of his nose, lips, and chin.

What have I done?

How could he have allowed himself to love both of these women so completely? Hurting Frankie was unforgiveable. She was his sunshine—so warm and sweet and funny. But why couldn't he get Patrice out of his system?

Garrison raised his face to the showerhead.

It was time to stop kidding himself. Patrice was his aspirational woman. She represented everything he wanted and worked to achieve—the life he wanted, the respect his credentials demanded, the man he was making of himself. Plus, she needed him. He was always there for her. He was deeply wounded when their relationship ended. He was determined to have her, despite her mother's ignorant prescriptions of class and color; suppressing the idea that maybe he needed or wanted her, as friends had accused, to complete his own idyllic class and color prescriptions—that whole African American arrival motif.

No, my love for her is real! He loved her selflessly. He had to be honest. She was a part of him, and that is the way he wanted it. She was the princess to his prince; the queen to his king in every way. There was nothing more important than that to a man like him. He committed to repairing the damage he had caused Frankie. Her friendship meant the world to him, and he would find a way.

Reconstituted, Garrison reached for the soap and bathed vigorously. He still felt like shit, but at least he had made a decision. Finally. He stepped out of the shower, wrapping the thirsty cotton towel around his waist. Doing so, he chuckled, reminded of how Frankie insisted on air-drying as part of her obsessive campaign against dry skin.

Damn! Who am I kidding?!

The 15 seconds it took him to dry off was like a montage of his life with Frankie. The first time he saw her; how he was drawn to her. Like a hunter, he used instincts he didn't know he had to find, befriend, and make her love him. She fed a hunger in Garrison he didn't fully understand. His body, mind, and soul responded involuntarily to her. He saw his children's spirits in her smile and their cherubic little faces in hers.

"Shiiiittttt!" he shouted, snapping the towel with such force, the shower rod and curtain fell with a clamor.

Naked, Garrison swiped a patch of steam from the mirror revealing his reflection.

"King huh," he muttered.

With Francine, he felt like a *god*!

***

Garrison sat on the floor, his back flush against the tub, welcoming the stimulation of the cold marble tile and porcelain chilling his hot skin. After an indiscernible amount of time, he stood and repositioned the rod and curtain in frustration, as if it held culpability in his confusion. One thing was clear. He could hear Erykah Badu's sultry twang wafting down the hall, *"... You betta call Tyrooooone. Call 'im! Tell him c'mon help you get yo shit..."*

9

Francine's medicine had kicked in. Her haze was jarred by the announcement:

"Now boarding first class only. First-class passengers, please make your way to the gate for boarding," the official voice said into the intercom.

She gathered her carry on and neck pillow and made her way through the other passengers to the front. She handed the attendant her boarding pass.

"Good evening, Dr. Carty. Thank you for flying with us." Francine returned the greeting.

First class really makes a difference, she thought as she walked through the corridor to enter the aircraft. The flight attendant checked her seat assignment at the entrance and escorted her to her seat.

"I'll take your luggage, Dr. Carty. My name is Heather, and I'll be taking care of you on your flight. Would you like a beverage while we continue to board?" Heather asked.

"Thank you, Heather, no," Francine felt compelled to let helpful Heather down gently.

Finally settled in her seat, Francine closed her eyes to relax while the flight boarded for another 30 minutes.

The final months of the semester had taken her for quite a ride. Her spring break trip home had come just in time to ground and stabilize her for what was to come. She was offered both fellowships. After countless consultations with Robbi and Ursula, they all agreed that she should accept The Search and request a deferred acceptance of the Sherman. The Search, albeit fraught with a good deal of uncertainty with the revelation of Roseline as Chase, was a once-in-a-lifetime opportunity. She could not let that stand in the way.

Thankfully, the grant was administered by members in the host country—in this case Ghana. Francine accepted The Search in writing, per the acceptance letter that followed the conversation. The letter also instructed her that all further interactions regarding the award must be confidential and made directly with the third-party administrators, until the completion of the grant. This meant Francine's requisite handwritten thank-you notes (with pints of Carty Tea) were her last correspondence with Mercer, Fortley, and Lashley regarding The Search. Roseline must have known this when she dropped the Chase bomb. But why would she even want Francine to know? Roseline could have carried on as if Chase and Zora had never happened.

Initially relieved, Frankie grew suspicious that it wasn't over. She recalled Robbi's admonishing her to be strategic so she followed Roseline's lead for now and focused on preparations to leave the country. As for the Sherman, it could not be deferred but did allow for a variable start date within the awarding academic year, allowing Francine to extend her study to 18 months. Her request to delay the start date was granted to begin funding at the close of The Search. This meant she would need to begin The Search almost immediately upon the end of the semester.

It also meant she needed to close out a few other things. Ursula gave up her downtown apartment and agreed to take over Francine's lease. She was approaching tenure review and could stand to be in a quiet setting as she prepared her dossier. It would also allow her better management of her budget. The Hansons were happy to have another reliable academic as a tenant and were familiar with Ursula as a frequent visitor. Presenting them with a tenant without a month's payment missed worked to smooth the ruffled feathers over the red wall. Francine restored it to the original color before Ursula moved in. Despite her casting off her social status at times, Ursula would always be a woman of upper-class tastes and the red wall had always perplexed her.

Francine posted an ad to sell her car for a whopping $1,500. She left three boxes of winter clothes with Ursula, packed her lightweight clothes in one large suitcase, and took home her Bennie and Winnie classics. Her parents threw her a lavish going-away dinner party Saturday night with only a faint aftertaste of maybe-this-will-catapult-her-career. It was good to spend time with her old friends. Ursula made the trip and spent a good deal of time stealing away in conversation with Mrs. Carty. Francine assumed their closeness was an effort for Ursula to piece together more of the mystery that was her mother.

Everyone insisted on marking her departure. Earl invited her and the other bartenders over to his place for a decadent dinner and evening of raucous laughter over liquid refreshments as they spilled the beans about their customers.

Francine's best tipper, Mr. Byron Sellers, insisted on gifting her with round trip upgrades to first class as his bon voyage gift.

"You're the best, Byron," Francine thanked him over drinks during her last shift.

"You don't want to be on an overseas flight stuck in coach. It's the least I could do. Plus, I'm gonna miss you, Francine. You're damned good company."

"Mr. Sellers, you're no slouch either." She gave him a big hug.

***

Francine had stressed about returning to work at the bar and facing Byron after Roseline revealed herself to be Chase. But her worry was completely unnecessary. Byron reminded her that he is, as she often referred to him, "Byron the Billionaire, telecommunications guru" and, with a raised eyebrow and amused smirk, waited for Francine to connect the dots. Two beats later, Francine realized he knew about her stint as Zora and—gasp!—Roseline as Chase!

Of course he knew. Byron had unprecedented access to phone, internet records, transcripts, etc. And he most likely used that access to keep track of the woman he loved.

"Look, Francine. I'm not looking to hurt anybody. I got my own problems," Byron said patting her shaking hand. "When I realized you knew Rose and remembered what you did on your last job, I just put two and two together. Now, it didn't occur to me at first, you being a professor and all. But I *know* my ex. I'm a pretty traditional guy, so once we came home and grew up, the marriage was doomed. We just wanted different things. It was only ugly on the inside—the agony, you know? It wasn't a messy divorce. I still love her, and I check up on her from time to time. It's wrong to do it *this* way, I know, and maybe even a little pathetic, but hey," he shrugged. "She couldn't care less if she never saw me again. But folks like me, people in love, do inappropriate things sometimes." Byron swirled his drink, then finished it in one tilt.

Francine had poured him a double, speechless and trembling.

"Francine, listen!" Byron said firmly, in full CEO mode now. "You are fine. No one is going to hurt you with this. I certainly don't have any business looking. Rose—I don't know what the hell she's been on all these years." His tone softened, "You think your little Chase-Zora scenario was weird, I've heard and seen far worse. Actually, it was a little sad. I honestly don't know what to think. Maybe I should have kept that info to myself, huh?"

"No, no. I'm glad you told me. Okay, so, nothing to fear from you, but what's Roseline up to? You know her! She knows I'm Zora. She was who had spoken to me in Portuguese, both as Chase *and* Roseline," Francine pleaded for direction.

"No idea, hon. But, I will say this. Rose is not the type of person to harm anyone unless you come for her first. You'll be fine. You were good to Chase," he laughed heartily then suddenly shifted into a more somber stance.

"But seriously, if anything does come up, here's how to reach me, from anywhere." Byron dug into his wallet for a two-sided card and placed it into the palm of her hand. It was his personal contact information on one side and initials on the other.

"I won't hurt her, but I *can* get you out of any trouble if you need it," he collected himself to greet two colleagues who entered the bar. They had a round, then left for their 7 p.m. dinner reservations in the restaurant. He never mentioned it again—a gentleman after all.

***

Frankie had completely zoned out as usual. The plane began its taxi on the runway. Tears welled up as she stared out of the window and recalled Garrison's final plea for forgiveness at her place weeks before. It was a terrible spectacle. Even Ursula, upon passing his sad sappy self on campus, felt badly for him. After the fallout over his romp with Patrice, they didn't speak for days. Francine buried her pain long enough to get through the week, reserving the weekend to cry and curse him. She was a murky cauldron of pain, jealousy, and self-loathing. She cried heaving gut tears intermittently for two days. She was dedicated both to mourning the relationship wholeheartedly and limiting the time she gave to that step in the process.

As she internally predicted, he showed up at her door. It was the closing hours of her cry-fest, just after she had showered and eaten for the first time in 48 hours. The knock on her door was tentative. She peered through the peephole.

He sensed her on the other side, "Frankie, please let me in."

She opened the door, fortified by his apparent defeat. Without a word, she gestured for him to have a seat in the single armchair. He obliged. Francine walked barefoot to the kitchen and poured him a glass of water from the pitcher she kept in the fridge with sprigs of fresh mint. In a fluid movement, she placed a marble coaster on the table beside him, and atop it, the glass of water. Francine then seated herself in the red loveseat where she had, ironically, spent most of her weekend crying to her Stevie Wonder compilation. She raised her eyes to meet his. He watched her every move for some indication that all was not lost. Hers responded with a simple demand, *What?!*

The torture began and continued for two hours:

I'm sorry. I love you.

Why her!?

I don't know.

I love you. I want you.

You hurt me.

I need you. Let me in.

Why? Why! I can't trust you.

I'm sorry. What will it take? You are a part of me. I love you.

I love you.

I can't do this.

Please don't say that. I love you. I love you.

I wish you well.

Come back to me.

Exhausted, they made war and love as if it were the last time, then said a tearful, unresolved goodbye.

Francine shook her head as if doing so would expel the memory from her thoughts. Exhausted all over again, and lulled by the engines of the plane, she fell fast asleep.

***

Francine awoke almost having forgotten where she was. It was dark. She made her way to the aisle and the restroom. When she came out, she spotted Heather just outside the cockpit.

"Hi Heather. Sorry to bother you. Can you tell me what time it is?" Francine asked.

"Certainly, Dr. Carty. It's 11:30 p.m. eastern time. You slept through dinner. Can I offer you something?"

"Heather, thank you. Please, I am hungry. Would you bring me whatever you have?"

Francine was now very grateful for her first-class accommodations. She adjusted her seat to the upright position and turned on the overhead light to a dim setting to avoid disturbing her aisle companion. She didn't even recall anyone seated next to her before she drifted off to sleep. Heather returned with a covered plate.

The aroma was heavenly. "What would you like to drink?" Heather asked.

"I'll take cranberry and seltzer with a twist of lemon or lime, please." Francine requested her standby beverage when she was minding her medication. She lifted the silver dome cover to reveal a magnificent presentation of lobster thermidor. Francine gasped, then looked quizzically at Heather who had returned in record time with her cranberry spritzer,

"Compliments of Mr. Sellers," Heather smiled and handed Francine a small card. Francine sat in disbelief as she broke the seal to read the card.

You might not have realized it, but you've been a bright light during a dark time.

Bon appétit and cheers to brighter futures for both of us!

Byron

"Oh Byron, you shouldn't have," Frankie said aloud.

She blessed her food, and indulged.

As she finished her meal, she heard a faint voice, "You must be a VIP. The stuffed chicken breast wasn't bad, but now I'm feeling a little insulted!"

She looked down at the man laid out beside her. His seat was reclined, and he appeared to be asleep. He had a full, long, well-maintained head of mostly gray hair worn in locs, with a full mustache and beard, equally well coiffed. He chuckled through the gray hairs that circled his lips as he uprighted his seat. He popped a mint in the circle of gray and twisted on his overhead light.

"Zechariah Johns," he said with a smile and nod, offering his hand.

Francine smiled at her cabin-mate. Amidst all of his hair, she noticed brown freckles a hint darker than his remarkably smooth skin and thick, lush black eyelashes shading youthful shining eyes.

Why was beautiful thick hair and lashes wasted on men, she wondered.

"Francine Carty," she said in return, shaking his hand. "I apologize if my late meal disturbed you."

"You apologize? How do you expect anyone to sleep through that shell cracking and cream dripping all over the place," he complained in jest.

Francine had to laugh. "I would offer you my last bite, but I had not planned to share. Now, I really don't think I will," she teased as she placed another forkful in her mouth.

"Well, I appreciate your candor," Mr. Johns said. "Did you finish off the Cristal?"

Francine laughed out loud, then quieted herself, "Mr. Johns! You're going to get me in trouble with Heather. She's accommodating and all, but I'll bet she runs a tight ship!"

"Ol' Heather's alright. We're the only two awake up here. You hear all that snoring? These people could use some time in a steam chamber. You too."

Francine laughed again, "What is with you!? I do *not* snore."

"Oh, yes you do! It's not too bad, though. Nothing some time off the sauce and a humidifier won't take care of," he said looking at her matter-of-factly.

"You are unbelievable." Francine finished the last two bites of her lobster and childishly chided, "mmm mmm mmm," as she dabbed the corners of her mouth with the cloth napkin and pushed the call button for Heather to retrieve the place setting.

"I saaaaid my stuffed chicken breast was *just fine*!" an amused Mr. Johns said in response.

"Heather, please, would you bring me a glass of whatever Ms. Carty is having?"

Heather expertly delivered on both requests sharing a smirk with Mr. Johns.

Francine observed the darker hue of the drink brought to Mr. Johns, "*That*, sir, is not what I'm having."

"Well, maybe you should. You had a very fitful sleep," he reported with sincere concern.

Over the next several hours, a few drinks, snacks, and breakfast, Francine and Mr. Johns, got acquainted. She told him about her grant, the breakup with Garrison, her feelings of limbo in her professional pursuits and hopes for the grant to serve as the bridge to her dreams. He shared his decision to "uproot" from a successful medical research career on the West Coast to relocate to rural Ghana where he operates a thriving medicinal herbs farm and presents his research at international conferences a few times annually. In a moment of reckless abandon, she even confided in him about her Fibro, to which he went into full physician mode, ordering hot tea, admonishing her for their drinking, inquiring about the hour of her last dose. Sensing Francine's icy withdrawal, he cautiously invited her to consult him with interest in herbal treatments. He understood that the side effects often discourage sufferers from staying on task with their meds. Having already developed an unexpected kinship with Dr. Johns, Francine forgave the transgression and actually engaged a full discussion of treatment modifications using herbs. Zechariah was relieved and generously obliged. The conversation eventually moved on to less weighty topics.

As the flight approached its end, Francine had made her first friend in Ghana. Zech, as he insisted she address him, gave her three local contact numbers and his address on the farm with an open invitation. They made their way through customs together, Zech as her expert guide for non-West African travelers and protection from the tip baiters. For an elder statesman, Zechariah had a pretty commanding swagger. He stood about 6'3" in casual chic slacks and a dashiki made of high-quality cotton. More importantly, he wore the comportment of an expert in navigating the arrival process. Francine, on the other hand, was identified as an easy target for the tip baiters. Zech instructed her to stick by his side. He greeted the airport staff with a nonchalant belonging that allowed them to complete the process without incident. Once officially in the country, they bid farewell.

"Dr. Johns, thank you for the escort. I appreciate it. I typically travel very well, but I'm so excited I'm over here looking like it's my first rodeo." Francine wasn't accustomed to addressing her elders so casually, so she persisted in her formal address.

"No worries, Francine. The novelty will wear off in no time."

Francine felt remarkably compelled to hug her new friend, then hesitated.

"Oh, come on now, bring it in," he invited her. "You're going to be fine." He gave her a brief firm hug and flashed a bright smile that she hadn't fully appreciated under the night light of the aircraft. There was a sparkle in Zech's smile that comforted her. She felt safe with his friendship.

He was happy to have shepherded another African American across the threshold to the home of their ancestors. Zech hoped Francine would reach out soon. She reminded him of happier days.

"Let me know when you get settled. I know the city very well and travel back here from time to time. It has been a pleasure. Do keep in touch and keep well, Francine Carty!" He gestured toward the sign that donned her name in bold letters.

"Thank you, Dr. Johns. I'll be in touch!" she waved as he ducked into an SUV that pulled up curbside to collect him.

Francine took a look around as she finally stepped into the fresh air from the Kotoka International Airport in Accra, Ghana. It was just after nightfall there. After traveling all over the Americas, Asia, and Europe, Francine had finally made it to the Motherland. She hoped it would treat her well.

10

"Welcome, Professor!" the driver greeted Zech with a firm handshake and a pat on the back as he climbed into the back seat. They exchanged pleasantries.

Kwame routinely drove Zech who paid him well because not only could he navigate the changing Ghanaian terrain, he was good company for the two-hour ride.

"Thanks, Kwame. Let's go directly to the farm please," he said.

Zechariah's voice was a heavy rumble—smooth, distant but flooded with contentment. There was something about returning to Ghana that always relieved the tension of constant travel. His work and research sent him around the globe speaking at conferences, discussing what he called the "herbal solution" to scholars and laypeople alike. It could certainly be exhausting, but Ghana—his home for years now—was the ultimate balm.

You think I'd leave your side baby.
You know me better than that.

From the radio, Sade sang his mood. They loved that woman on the continent. Counted her as their own. He loved her too. She was the kind of timeless sexy that both comforted and aroused men young, old, and in-between. The breezy heat from the window rolled down halfway warmed Zechariah's face as he closed his eyes and allowed her words to wash him anew.

When you're on the outside baby and you can't get in.
I will show you, you're so much better than you know.

Zechariah knew he'd felt it. He'd spent too many years trying not to feel it again to not know that the emotion had finally risen tall in him. After so much time, it had finally revealed the possibility of freedom—a kind of emotional deliverance—after years of numbness and more years of waiting. What he hadn't figured out was why it had come. Why then? The trigger was clear. The woman on the plane. The one snoring and eating lobster. The one with the pains and the pills. The one whose aura was like hands reaching and searching for something. What was it about her?

I'll tell you you're right when you want
And if only you could see into me

Intrigue, for sure. That was the first wave to hit; the first feeling to show itself big in his mind.

The next, he found to be a bit strange, even for him. Zechariah felt protective of the woman—Francine—despite the fact that he'd just met her. Like he needed to defend her or help her stay out of her own way. She was definitely what Americans called "a free spirit," yet he was certain that she hadn't quite grasped that being a free spirit actually costs a person something.

Zechariah kept his eyes closed as the third and final wave of emotion hit him hard. Like a tsunami.

Familiarity.

This was the one he would have preferred to not experience. But Zechariah was long past avoidance in his journey. He knew he had to sit in it. Let it wash over him. Even let it pull him out into the depths if it meant he would be whole again.

Familiarity. Yes, he'd felt this intrigue and protectiveness many years before—with Meredith.

He'd also felt the stinging pain of realizing that none of it was enough.

***

"Let's go, Mer!"

"I ain't going nowhere with you," she said, nodding to the gangly boy, barely 18, with missing teeth and skin the color of compost.

The manchild wrapped the rubber tubing around Meredith's skeletal arm and tied it off in a tight knot.

"You need help, baby," Zechariah said, his eyes soft with compassion. His hair was a mass of black curls with graying temples. "Let me help you."

There were both men and women strewn about the room. The ones who were flying were obvious. Their eyes were glazed over as though they were seeing the glory of angels ascending to the heavens. Dribbles of saliva leaked from the corner of their mouths, an outward symbol of their complete relinquishment of their lives to the drugs. Those on the way down were balled up in fetal positions in the corners of the room, shaking and trying to ride out the free-fall into the pit of hell. There was even a toddler sitting in a blue-turned-black-from-dirt-and-grime Bumbo chair with his thumb in his mouth and a bottle filled with some kind of red juice clinched under his arm. Though the smell clearly indicated that the child's diaper had soiled days prior, the child didn't cry. The little boy just stared back at Zechariah with empty eyes filled with a resignation beyond his years.

His Meredith didn't belong there. She'd been an attorney in one of the top firms in the country. They'd met while she was still in law school and he was finishing up his Masters. She was the one who captured his soul, and they'd married quickly after both of their graduations. When he realized that she'd become addicted, he was determined to not give up on his jewel. He stood by her through several treatment programs, some of the best in L.A. And yet thousands of dollars and tears later, he still stood in a crack house in Long Beach begging her to try to get clean one more time.

The needle sank into her arm just as Zechariah ran toward his wife. The wall of muscle and flesh he slammed into on the way was the only thing that stopped him from yanking the needle out and dragging her away.

Of course, these dealers would have goons protecting their investments, he thought.

"Meredith, please! I know it hasn't been easy, but we can beat this!" He pleaded from behind the gangster's chest.

But Zechariah knew that she was halfway to glory by then. It was done.

"Mer?" his voice was low and graveling. Emotion caught in his throat. He needed to say it. Just let the words meet the air and become real. The goon stepped away, realizing that Zechariah had finally broken like all the others he'd seen come in with their capes on and hopes up.

"If you don't leave with me now, I'm gone. I won't be back."

He watched the eyes of the shell of his wife roll around in their sockets. Her head rocked back and forth like a broken pendulum.

Zechariah wiped the lone and final tear that escaped his eyes. He looked around at the human carnage once again and shook his head.

Then he left.

***

The images in his head startled Zechariah awake. He'd gone deep this time. Deeper than he had in a long while. Maybe it *was* time.

***

After a week of settling in, Francine had finally organized her research schedule. She'd confirmed interviews with members of several different families with ties to Nkrumah and would be spending time with them over the following weeks. The Search had opened many of the doors in advance to make the most of her time. At last, on the first Friday after her arrival, she decided to take a moment to just breathe and take in her space. She sat in a rattan rocking chair on the wraparound veranda of the beautiful guesthouse she would call home for the next nine months. As part of The Search grant, Francine was staying in housing normally set aside for ambassadors, near both the U.S. Embassy and the campus of Accra College of the Humanities where she would be doing her research. It was evening, and the sunset was the most amazing she'd ever seen. The sky almost seemed angry. Red streaks slammed drunkenly into the darkening horizon creating a purple haze that hovered over one part of the city. Yet even as she watched another one of God's masterpieces being created right before her eyes, she couldn't help but to drift inward in her thoughts. Specifically, how she planned to respond to Ursula's "urgent" email about what happened between Francine and Garrison.

> *Girl, this man is upset. You know he HAS to be if he's talking to me with even a little bit of civility. I actually feel sorry for him. What in the world happened between you two? He won't give me details. Just keeps saying that he needs to talk to you. That he messed up. Write me back. I already miss you entirely too much, Sis.*
>
> *U.*

What could she possibly say that would make any of it make sense? The annoying pain that she was trying so desperately to push down deep inside her kept pressing against her throat and threatening to expose her feelings with the sob that sat waiting for release. When the sky finally disintegrated into darkness, Francine moved her sentiments indoors. Sitting at the handcrafted desk that loomed large in the sitting room, she opened her laptop.

> *Hey Sis:*
>
> *I miss you too! I'm finally getting my sea legs here. What an amazing experience so far. I only*

hope I'm worthy of it. So yeah, about Garrison. Geesh, I mean, what do I say? The details are, in a way, embarrassing. I can't believe how stupid I was to even remotely believe that the relationship would come of something. The bottom line is, he hurt me. I almost feel like what he did, how he made me feel, changed the trajectory of my whole life (dramatic much?). LOL.

But seriously, I'm so angry. There's this rage simmering like boiling water, hot underneath my skin. That's why I can't talk to him. I've deleted every email he's sent so far. I guess I feel like any word from him will trigger a bubbling over that will scold me and everyone in any emotional proximity to me. And of course, I can't afford for that to happen here. Gotta keep my head in the game, ya know?

Once I figure out how this international phone app works, let's chat for real, for real.

Muah!

Ms. Carty

Francine was tired of thinking about Garrison. The whole thing exhausted her. *For goodness sake, I'm in Ghana,* she thought as she turned off her laptop and stripped off the wrap skirt she wore around her hips. Although she would eventually share the space with two other yet-to-arrive grantees from other fellowships, Francine was living in a mansion compared to her tiny guesthouse apartment in Mt. Airy. The lodging came with a driver, cook, and housekeeper—that was just the way things were among the middle class in Ghana. The generators in the area where she stayed were consistent, which meant air conditioning and electricity were always in supply. The shops, restaurants, and nightclubs that were concentrated in the upscale neighborhood beckoned for her patronage. Francine was done wallowing in what might have been. She decided that it was finally time for her to take in a breath of fresh air and release herself from the grasp of her past. It was time to forget it all and, as her mother and the Jack and Jill moms used to whisper to each other as though no one could hear their giggles about their unofficial mothers' "retreats," let her hair down a bit.

As Francine removed the tank top she wore and padded her way to the shower, she glanced down at the sofa table that was positioned behind a grand leather couch. *Zechariah Johns, MD, PhD.*

"He certainly was interesting," she said to herself as she smiled and tossed the card into her purse. Couldn't hurt to have someone to call, right? Just in case.

11

It was almost 10 p.m. and Francine wore a beautiful strapless fit and flare dress that she'd picked up from the dressmaker she'd met the day after she arrived.

When Francine landed in Accra, she was surprised to see so many people dressed in Western clothing. About town, Francine observed the men wearing basic slacks or jeans, tailor-made Western shirts with touches of traditional designs along the pocket or collar or cuffs and European-looking dress shoes or nice leather sandals—which Francine later learned were called slippers there. But on Friday, she noticed, most everyone dressed in clothes made from traditional cloths, colors, and patterns. Joseph, her driver, explained that Traditional Fridays was the equivalent of casual Fridays in the U.S. It was a way for Ghanaians to celebrate their centuries-old heritage in textiles and to keep the industry alive as more and more people donned cheaper Western clothes they could buy off the racks. He recommended a dressmaker and took Francine to see her the very next day.

Joseph greeted the young woman with a hug, then said something to her in Twi. A girl of about 9 years old offered them glasses of water. After 30 minutes of measuring and selecting a few fabric designs, Joseph and Francine headed out to their next errand. The dressmaker handed Francine a business card that read:

Ju'fedi, Elegance is our Hallmark.

Amazingly, the dressmaker assured Francine her dresses would be ready in only a few days. They were, and they fit magnificently.

"Madame, the dress is very beautiful!" Joseph complimented her as she came down the stairs. "I will tell Judith her work is good."

Francine thanked Joseph for both the compliment and introducing her to the talented dressmaker.

Joseph appeared to be close to Francine's age, so she trusted his recommendation for a spot called the Bourbon Room. It was a steady mix of Ghanaians and internationals.

"Perfect," Francine declared.

"What time would you like me to collect you, Madame?" Joseph inquired.

"Hmm, let's say around 12:30?" he said, not giving her a chance to answer.

Ten minutes later, Francine stepped out of the car. The Bourbon Room was a two-story building with outdoor seating encircling the front and sides of the place. A man unclipped a velvet rope, giving her access to the outdoor seating area. Francine followed him through a large foyer where people lingered on cell phones, in romantic pairs, or clusters of friends out for a night on the town. Sheer red, gold, and green drapes dramatically clasped at each side, revealing a door shaped like a huge bourbon tumbler. Nickel letters—"BR"—cleverly shaped the ornate handle to the door.

"Welcome to the Bourbon Room, enjoy." The man left her in the capable care of a host, who invited her to select a seat at a small table or at the bar. She chose to sit at the bar, deciding she'd appear less alone—the last feeling she needed to experience right then.

The bartender greeted her, "Welcome to the Bourbon Room. My name is Foli. Is this your first time joining us?"

"Yes, it is. This place is fabulous." Francine took in the supper club vibe: high-backed banquettes, assorted table sizes for two, four, and larger parties. The crowd was definitely upscale and international. About 40 percent of the people seemed to be from other parts of the world, of every tongue and hue. The ladies wore colorful cocktail dresses. Francine liked that these women celebrated all shapes and sizes. It probably helped that there were dressmakers all over the place—no ill-fitting, too small here, too large there ensembles about the place. Francine noticed that the men really seemed to invest equally, if not more, into their clothes. They dressed in expertly tailored shirts and slacks that really flattered the physique. She sipped her soda, taking in the environment appreciatively.

She placed an order for a plate of kelewele and a flavorful spicy rice and beans dish, familiar menu items that the cook, Nana, had prepared for her earlier in the week.

"Ah, you have been eating well. No cooking like this in the States, eh?" Foli chided.

"I'm sure it's somewhere. Philadelphia has a significant West African population. Maybe I can learn to make it while I am here!" Francine suggested.

"This dish is not for the fainthearted. There are people born here who don't make this dish well. Our chef is very good--like your Southern soul food. Cooking from the heart," Foli said and excused himself to greet new arrivals at the other end of the bar. His greeting shifted from English to French then Ewe without skipping a beat.

It sure tasted like soul food, Francine thought. Foli was very good at his job. Working at the Bourbon Room required him to know a little about a lot and to learn it rapidly. He had probably seen all kinds of comings and goings. The return of the band interrupted her observations. They announced their last set for the evening, playing an assortment of lounge hits for the crowd in Portuguese, English, and French to showcase the vocalist. Then they played a couple of Fela hits to ignite the crowd and showcase the musicians. Finally, the quintet closed with a few Congolese favorites that brought the crowd to the dance floor, getting the party started before the DJ took over.

By this time, Francine had finished her dinner and made a few friends at the bar with whom, against her better judgment, she had joined in at least two rounds of drinks. But tonight was a night to throw caution to the wind. No Garrison, no "Chase," no problems—except for the fact that she had been pretty regimented about taking her meds since arriving in Ghana. She knew full well that she should not drink alcohol, but desperate times …

As the DJ took over, the crowd turned over. The new folks were slightly less successful entrepreneurs, government/corporate workers, and more of the entitled/pampered with money-to-burn set. Intrigued, Francine thought *when in Rome* and ordered another round.

Tye, one of the guys she'd met at the bar, stuck around while his friends left for the night. It was about 11:45, so Francine had a little more time to spend before she was to meet Joseph outside to drive her home. She and Tye found a table near the dance floor. The place was quickly filling to capacity seating so a party of three invited themselves to share their table. At that point, Tye, a gangly Brit in his late 30s, was about as bad off as Francine and enjoying the high. The DJ put on a broad appeal of R&B and hip-hop classics that kept everyone on the dance floor—*Shake It Fast*, followed by Nelly's *Hot in Herre,* then 50 Cent's *In Da Club.* As 50 Cent's popular baseline began, the DJ called for a "boooonuuus rouuuuuund" and all the servers topped off anyone on the dance floor with a drink in their hands for as long as the song played.

Francine was feeling the effects of the alcohol and prescription drug mixture. First it was the exhilarating high—she'd always been a jovial and affectionate drunk. On the dance floor, she felt as if she were floating. Tye seemed to drift farther and farther away at the start of the bonus round, eventually becoming invisible. The dance floor was so packed, Francine had to move in step with the momentum of the crowd. It reminded her of the Labor Day weekend she spent at the Caribbean Day parade in Brooklyn. Only it was darker, indoors, and had different music. Her new dance partner's face appeared to be distorting in slow motion. Her limbs felt numb although she knew she was moving or maybe … he was moving her? They were dancing so close. Francine couldn't tell what was what anymore and embraced the free fall escape. She felt her head swoon and her feet seemed to be floating six inches above the floor now. She gave up and in.

The party went on. The dance floor remained crowded all night. The cocktails flowed. On the second level that overlooked the dance floor, there was more seating, more bars, more entitlement, more money. Overlooking the DJ booth was the VIP area and the DIP room. The owners, celebrities, and investors could access the VIP for private seating, etc. The DIP aka Diplomatic Immunity in Progress space was another animal. In there, a kind of debauchery that is frowned upon in Ghana in general unfolded for international guests. Guests needed to show international credentials to enter, at the very least. In general, weapons, recording devices, and discussion of politics were strictly prohibited. But in the Bourbon Room DIP, anything goes. Wait staff dressed in expensive lingerie. The room was soundproof, had a private DJ, food prep, and even a separate exit. This night, the DIP was filled to capacity with about 45 foreign government officials, military, and civilians of high status, including trust fund mid-lifers. Outsiders would never expect what unfolded there on a nightly basis and that night offered the usual prohibited contraband: weapons, political deals, and hard drugs. In addition to this, there was the typical socializing and dancing.

***

In the DIP room, an inebriated couple huddled in a corner, nursing drinks, kissing, and dancing occasionally to a Beyoncé's triple play of *Partition*, *Rocket,* and *Blow*. The woman slowly began a striptease for her partner, who was taken a bit off guard and tried to rebuff her. The woman easily dismissed him, quickly scanning the room for another interest. There were several. Now clad only in her bra, granny panties, and flip-flop kitten-heeled sandals, the woman offered a clumsy but sincere burlesque performance that everyone assembled to watch half-heartedly. The DJ, in jest, played *Don't Cha* by the Pussycat Dolls and Busta Rhymes.

Don't cha wish your girlfriend was hot like me?
Don't cha wish your girlfriend was a freak like me?
Don't cha?
Don't cha?

In a matter of minutes, there was an inept belly dance with a general. Sweat beaded both her red-hot face and torso during a slightly more impressive lap dance for a former head of state who'd put paper currency in the waistband of her now loose granny panties clinging to her sweaty bottom.

"It's so hot!" she kept slurring.

Stumbling over to the bar, she reached behind it retrieving a can of whipped cream. She sprayed and smeared her stomach and back with whipped cream to cool herself down, "Ooh, that feels so good."

Adding cocktail cherries from the bar, she challenged onlookers to retrieve them from her navel and cleavage. Oddly, tears streamed from her eyes, but she seemed oblivious to them. As the song ended, the room gave a ridiculing applause. The DIP was a tough crowd who'd seen it all.

One of the men helped her gather her things. Propping her up in the corner, he covered her with a linen tablecloth from behind the bar. As the last of the onlookers resumed their activity, the woman vomited onto the tablecloth and slipped in and out of consciousness. Then she passed out completely. The bartender casually picked up the house phone. "Cleanup," he said and then replaced the receiver on the hook.

Just another night in the DIP.

***

Francine awakened slowly to streaks of sun streaming through the closed window shutters in her bedroom. She tried to lift her head, but it seemed too heavy for her neck. It dropped like a medicine ball into the pillow. What felt like hours later, she heard the rattle of the housekeeper opening the shutters to the full sun.

"You need to get up, Miss. I've brought your tea, and your shower is ready."

The woman waited for Francine to respond.

"Madame, please!"

For the life of her, Francine could not remember the housekeeper's name or much else for that matter. *Who is this woman?*

"Who's in my apartment?" she managed to groan, although she was going for a yell.

Francine's uncooperative body lay on the bed, her brain willing it to obey. After a few minutes, she was able to flop her hands and feet and move her legs a bit.

What is that horrible smell, she thought, moaning with disgust.

She had the worst case of cottonmouth since graduate school. Francine bent her arm to scratch her head, but instead of the soft, fluffy coils that always attracted admiring stares, her hand met what felt like rice crispy treats.

"What the devil?" she mumbled.

Francine managed to turn onto her side and realized the trouble she was having wasn't only due to her sleeping limbs, but the fact that she appeared to be stuck. She pulled the sheet, peeling it away from her skin. Scared to death, she found the strength to upright herself and stumble to the bath, knocking over and spilling something with her foot.

Her eyes adjusted to the mirror to reveal a frightful vision. She looked as if she had Crisco shortening all over her body.

The shower the housekeeper started began to steam up the room. Francine fought to focus so she could see what was wrong with her. She felt her skin and shrieked at the dry, crackly wrapping it had become.

Oh my God, she thought, *I shouldn't have drunk last night. I've never reacted this way before.* In a panic and on the verge of tears, she managed to get into the shower. Francine let the hot water trickle over her, hating that the water pressure was so low. Before she could think, she noticed cloudy water filling up in the tub to her ankles. Not able to fully bend, she used her toes to release the stopper to let the water out. And why was it so cloudy? Her toes met something mushy, definitely not the stopper.

Francine managed to leap out of the shower. In doing so, she had loosened something between her legs. The water swirled down a bit, then stopped. She saw something red. That didn't immediately shock her as she was near the end of her menstrual cycle. But that didn't explain what was stopping up the drain. She looked around the bathroom and grabbed the toilet brush. Reluctantly, she used it to fish out whatever had slowed the drain. The cloudy water swirled hypnotically, as she watched to see what would be revealed. When she'd clearly identified the culprit, she scooped up the mashed mess and sat it on the sink, relieved that it wasn't something more gross or scary. The shower had gone cold while she waited for the water to drain. Francine looked at herself in the now clear mirror and barely recognized the slimy cloudy mess of a woman with what she now identified as vomit in her hair. Perplexed by the image, she looked back to the sink at what had clogged the drain: three and a half cocktail cherries.

***

Francine frantically wracked her brain to try to recall what happened the night before. Stepping back into the cold shower, she scrubbed her body and shampooed her hair vigorously, crying the entire time. The last thing she could remember was dancing in the packed crowd. Wait! How did she get out of there? Did she get sick in bed? And what was this greasy slime all over her body? After a good 20 minutes, Francine emerged from the bathroom, with a mouthful of mouthwash. Spotting the tea, she went back to spit out the mouthwash, rinsing again with a water.

Back at her bedside, she poured herself a cup of tea and sat wrapped in a towel on the bed. Francine still felt like she was moving in slow motion. She checked her phone for the time. *It can't be 2:30*, she thought. She pulled the smelly, sticky sheets from the bed.

These are disgusting. I have to wash them myself. She was beyond embarrassed. Once she had balled up the sheets and piled them by the door, Francine noticed the overturned wastebasket of vomit spilled on the floor.

This was too much. She used a hand towel to clean up the mess, poured the vomit into the toilet, and did her best to rinse the wastebasket. Finally, she sat at the edge of the bed and took a gulp of tea. Feeling as calm as chamomile could bring her, she exhaled a deep sigh. As she reached for the tea setting to refill her cup, she noticed a small white envelope on the tray.

Francine started to open it, but first grabbed her favorite linen sundress from the still only partially unpacked suitcase and pulled her hair back into a puff. Finally, she sat down on the bare mattress to read the note.

One word: *Come.*

At the bottom of the stationary was an unfamiliar address, but the name she absolutely recognized: Dr. Zechariah Johns.

12

"Drink it down fast."

Zechariah handed Francine a coffee mug that read *LA Lakers 1988 NBA Champions*. She'd almost forgotten he was American. Thick clouds of steam poured out of the lavender-scented potion as she hesitated. Could she trust him? Could she trust anyone?

Zech saw her fear and understood. She couldn't have known how covered she was so far away from home. There were eyes everywhere, observing her from a distance, always watching even when her night of debauchery took a humiliating turn. In fact, if she wasn't protected, there's a strong possibility that, in the wrong hands, she could have been dead by the morning or nearly so. But again, she didn't know all of that. And he sensed it wasn't the time to tell her.

"You are safe," Zech said, his voice a salve on a wound she couldn't identify.

Francine's eyes welled as she continued to search her brain for answers. How did she get back home? What happened? Why did she even bother coming when he called after her? She supposed it was instinctual. She'd gotten that "guardian" vibe from him even on the plane. Unfortunately, she didn't realize she'd need guarding so soon.

She took a sip and her body warmed. The relief was almost immediate. She drank down the rest and laid back on the side of the sectional that jutted out into the middle of the nearly bare room. For the first time since she'd awakened, the moments of vertigo had gone. As she looked around, her orientation returned to her like some kind of game of restoration domino in her brain—bit by bit, with every glance and movement.

"Woah. That was fast. What is this?"

Without responding, Zechariah sat down directly across from Francine in a wide sofa chair lined with African engravings along the arms and legs. He sipped his own cup of tea and watched her for several minutes. His face was unreadable.

His was a work/live space. What he referred to as his research studio was actually a large greenhouse connected to his living quarters, intricately designed with irrigation hoses and lighting along the floors.

A greenhouse in this climate? Francine thought as he gave her an abbreviated tour of the place when she first arrived.

"To control the conditions."

He'd responded as though he knew what she was thinking. As if the question was one that came up often.

The open-concept great room where the two sat across from each other, exuded calm. Like a spa, only better. The scents of herbs and spices surrounded her. As a matter of habit, Francine looked around for a television when she first entered the space. She didn't know why she always did that. It was just her thing. Maybe the presence of a television corresponded to a person's level of pretentiousness in her mind. She'd had one too many discussions with academics who'd sworn off television and held anyone who dared to argue its cultural value in contempt.

No TVs.

Having not visited other parts of the home, Francine actually didn't know this for sure but she sensed it to be true. He came off to her, not pretentious like the others, but as simply a man who had too much to do and think about. His layers were many and it probably, she thought, never even occurred to him to get a television.

"How are you feeling?" Zechariah asked finally. His words were genuine.

"Honestly?" she asked.

"That's the only way to answer," he said with a smile.

She returned a half-smile back to him.

"Scared."

He nodded.

She wanted to ask him if he knew what happened to her. Her memories of the night before were like faded Polaroid snapshots of some other person's exploits. There were parts she remembered—dancing, Beyoncé, drinking—but not much else. But the ache in her body and soul told her that there was much, much more to the story.

Zechariah sat his mug on the small, circular end table with matching engravings next to him and leaned in with his elbows on his knees.

"Do you remember what I admonished on the plane?"

In that moment she didn't and said as much.

He sat back again and shook his head.

"Don't be the arbiter of your own demise, dear."

Francine was offended. She didn't know this man. She didn't know anything about him. How dare he cast judgment on her? How dare he suggest that somehow she was unequipped to manage her own life? She stood up and looked around for the intercom. She would call Joseph and tell him to take her back to the house immediately.

"Sit," Zechariah said.

Francine refused.

Zech chuckled. She was a fiery one, for sure. He knew that the "dear" was patronizing, but he enjoyed riling her up a bit. She wore her American-Black-Feminist-for-Life badge all over her countenance and he found it … well, like everything else about her … intriguing.

"Please call Joseph. I'd like to leave."

"Okay," he said.

"Okay."

Zechariah stood up to call the driver when a rhythmic melody from a tenor sax escaped Francine's bag still sitting on the couch. She reached down and pulled her cell phone out of the side pocket, swiping her finger across the screen. It was an in-app message notification from Byron.

> *Hey. Call me as soon as you can. Don't worry about the time. It's urgent. –Byron*

"Is everything alright?" Zech asked, his voice measured. He was still headed to the intercom to ask Joseph to bring her car around.

Francine had already opened up the international calling app and dialed Byron's number. She gave him a look that said, *Wait.*

"Frankie," Byron answered after only two rings. His voice was strange but she couldn't pinpoint what was different about it.

"Hey, what's up, what's going on?"

"Are you sitting down?"

Francine's heart began to race. *Why do people say that? As if you can't pass out or have a heart attack while seated.* The familiar pressure returned to her chest as anxiety stood waiting to push her into a full-on panic attack. Zechariah watched her closely as he quietly slipped back into the kitchen and began heating up more water on the small gas range. He opened a cabinet with shelves to the ceiling, filled with glass bottles and vials of various sizes. He took off the second shelf, two medium-sized bottles—one with green leaves soaking in a thick gel substance and the other with brown roots. Francine sat down.

"Yes. I'm seated. You're scaring me. What's going on?"

There was a long sigh before Byron responded. "I'm going to send something to your phone."

***

Francine stared at the woman on the screen. She looked like her. Wore the same beautifully patterned dress and open-toed sandals as her. Her hair was styled exactly like hers. Her lips, eyes, nose … all her. But Francine was having a hard time reconciling what she was seeing on that screen with what she believed about herself and her own character only 24 hours before.

Horrified didn't begin to describe how she felt. It was her fifth time watching the video, this time with Zechariah. He didn't seem moved by it, a fact she wasn't sure how to take. She'd debated whether to show it to him at all, and he'd even offered not to watch it but the truth was she needed confirmation. She needed someone else to stand next to her and confirm that this awful embarrassment was actually happening. Plus, after all that happened last night, she'd somehow ended up tucked neatly in her bed with a note from him saying to come to his home the next day. *He must know something*, she thought. *And I must be careful.*

"I don't know what to say." Francine's face was still wet with the tears that poured from her eyes when she'd first received the video from Byron.

"There is nothing to say," he said as he handed her another cup of the steamy potion he'd given her earlier. She hesitated again.

"It's an herbal remedy for stress and anxiety. It also helps with the digestive system. Some of the elders in the villages even give it to new mothers to help their milk come in. The Akan have used it for at least a millennia."

Comforted only slightly by his explanation but remembering how she'd felt after the first cup, she drank the warm concoction. And just as methodically as before, the beat of her heart slowed and a tingling sensation traveled down her spine, her buttocks, her legs, right into her toes.

"Tell me what you know," she said. Her eyes searched his. For the first time in a long time, Zech felt compelled to look away from someone. But he didn't.

"Joseph called Kwame, who was bringing me home from a late meeting."

Confusion filled Francine's face.

"It's a small world, these drivers," Zechariah said.

Aaaahhhh, Francine thought.

"Seems as though he went back to collect you as agreed, but no one seemed to know where you were," he continued.

"But why did he call your driver, why reach out to you?"

Zechariah ignored the question and continued, "When he said you were missing, I made some calls. After I got the information I needed, I sent Joseph in and asked him to bring you home."

Francine dropped her head. Shame overran her heart and mind. *What must this man think of me?*

"Do you remember now what I warned you about on the plane?"

Francine searched her mind, infinitely clearer than when she arrived. She looked up.

"About drinking and the Fibro medicine?"

He nodded.

"Poor chemical interactions in the body can have the most devastating effects. Physically, mentally, and spiritually."

Francine dropped her head again. She knew better. She was so careful back home. And now her first week away, she'd screwed up this badly.

"I'm going to lose everything," she said.

She looked up again at Zechariah, hoping that he would tell her differently. Praying that there would be some easy way out of this mess she'd created. Byron told her that the video had not yet gone viral in the States and that he would easily stop it from doing so. But unfortunately, it had already come to the attention of nearly all the people who mattered, namely, Roseline Mercer and The Search fellowship committee. Roseline had reached out to Byron for help—something that pained her to do but was necessary to protect the reputation of the network. Byron, willing to help both Roseline and Francine—but mostly Roseline—had already begun making his telecom billionaire moves to stop it from going any further. Nevertheless, the real damage had already been done. Her credibility as an educator and scholar was shot. *They must all be laughing at me.*

Zech, as was his way, didn't respond.

"Aren't you going to say something?" Francine said, her voice heavy with exhaustion and sadness.

"It will work itself out. These things always do."

***

The first room Francine was led to was considerably dark. The only light that shone was from a small window tucked away in the back upper corner. However, the place was far from a dungeon. The furniture was pure British elegance. Lattice work was carved into the teak feet of the coffee table and writer's desk. White tufted chairs beautifully contrasted with the floral patterns on two of the walls in the room. Whoever lived there was certainly someone with impeccable taste or enough money to hire someone with it.

"Have a seat, Ms. Carty. The ladies will be with you shortly."

Despite the exquisite art and furnishings around her, Francine's lungs felt like they were being held in a vice. The day after finding out about the video, she received a letter requesting a meeting with three named members of something called The Continental Committee (TCC). She'd referenced her online correspondences immediately and learned that TCC was the African contingency of the same network that Dean Mercer, Mrs. Fortley, and the other Search Fellowship committee members of WHUP belonged. Of course, she'd chatted casually with Ursula and even Garrison about all the assumed connections of the network—a reach that extended well outside higher ed. Ursula had even suggested that the First Lady was somehow connected to the group. But it wasn't until she was seated on tufted seats in some obscure wealthy neighborhood north of Accra, did Francine realize just how deep and wide the network really went.

"They are ready for you now."

The man, dressed in a uniform made from cloth with the TCC insignia imprinted in old-world script, had returned to escort her to the next room. Francine's insides shook. She walked in and was immediately directed to sit in the hot seat.

"Explain yourself," said Fosua Addo. She was the head of one of the largest generator manufacturing companies in Ghana and was not one to mince words. Plus, there was no need to bring anyone up to speed on the video. They all knew why they were there.

Francine tried to speak but the words wouldn't come out.

Another woman in the room, the only one who went by one name with no titles, Midim, spoke quickly. "You don't have anything to say? Do you not know the gravity of your actions?"

Francine found her voice. "Yes, I do. I want to say I'm deeply sorry for my actions. While there is absolutely no excuse for the behavior demonstrated in that video, you should know that some of what you see is the result of a dangerous interaction between the alcohol I consumed and prescription medications I was on for a minor illness."

Midim was a mystery. The only thing that Francine and Ursula could come up with was that she was the head of some large textile company in Togo but was deeply connected in Ghanaian politics. But these were all assumptions at best.

Mme. Addo shuffled through a file in front of her.

"This illness? Fibromyalgia, it is called?"

"Yes," Francine answered, silently thanking God that she'd decided to disclose her illness on her initial application.

The women looked at each other, but Francine could not decipher what they were clearly communicating to each other.

The third woman, Charlotte Botchwey, spoke next—mostly to the other women than to Francine. Her voice sounded like gravel and betrayed her youthful skin, revealing that she was truly the elder in the room.

"How will we explain this to the network? What if it gets out? How will this reflect on our work … us? Especially LaVaughn. She must be insulated from this."

Francine's face showed her confusion. *Who in the world is LaVaughn?*

The three women's eyes shone with something other than disgust for the first time since she'd arrived to the estate. They'd just realized how green Francine was. She didn't know anything. And that could be very good.

Mme. Addo closed the folder and looked at Francine for another moment before speaking. Of course, they'd already put a plan in place. They just needed to see the girl. Look at her face. Know what they were working with. Discern her true character.

"Here is what will happen going forward. Of course, we cannot name you as fellow. That is done."

Francine's heart sank.

"However, we will allow you to stay in Ghana for the remainder of your allotted time. We do not think it is a good idea for you to return home too soon. We don't want any leaks. Midim will take care of the officials, yes?"

Midim's nod was almost imperceptible.

"From your application, it looks as if you accepted the Sherman Fellowship also and that was scheduled to begin immediately after The Search, yes?"

"Yes," Francine said. Her mouth was dry. She held the woman's gaze mostly because if she looked away, she was scared that the room would start spinning.

"We strongly recommend that you contact the Sherman committee to see if you might advance the date for your work."

Francine's face finally registered the shock of what was happening.

Much like a choreographed dance, Mme. Botchwey picked up where Addo left off.

"Unfortunately, you will need to move out of the home you are currently living in as it is ambassador housing and well, we don't want the reputation of the place to be damaged. The video was available in our time zone for at least four hours online."

A tear pressed against the corner of her right eye. Francine willed it not to fall.

They handed off the dissemination of instruction again. "However, based on the recommendation of a …" Mme. Addo opened the folder quickly, then let fall again. " …Dr. Zechariah

Johns, we will allow you to keep your driver and will offer you assistance in finding another rental. You will have accommodations in my brother's hotel until the details are confirmed."

Mme. Botchwey spoke again, "Any questions?"

There was nothing left to say. Francine struggled to determine whether the result was good or bad—given the circumstances. Of course, it was bad that she'd lost The Search Fellowship, but she had a glimmer of hope that they understood. Or maybe they were just in mitigation mode. Whatever their motivations, they were willing to help her shift gears and she didn't expect that.

Francine shook her head. Speaking would likely cause her to crumble, and she needed to keep it together until she got into the car.

The three women nodded at each other. Another silent message.

"Good. Then we are done here," Midim said.

When Francine got back into her car she let the tears free fall. She'd ruined a good thing. *How will I ever regain their respect?*

"Where to, Ms. Carty?" Joseph asked.

Francine thought about it a bit. There was no point of rushing back to a house she'd have to move out of in two days. The weight of that was just too heavy. There were two people she definitely wanted to talk to. The first person was no shock to her. She needed to hear Robena's voice of reason. *What is my strategy now, Big Sis?* She'd call her later and run down everything though, if she knew her sister, Robbi probably already knew what happened.

The next person she desired to talk to took her totally by surprise.

"Please, take me to Dr. Johns, Joseph."

***

"I'm probably going to have to redo my proposal for the Sherman," Francine said as she sat on the dark wooden stools that lined the massive peninsula in Zech's kitchen. She was amazed at how comfortable she felt there in such a short time. His home, his presence soothed her. There was absolutely no tension in the air. Emotions, thoughts, energy, it all seemed to flow freely around and through the man, despite how much of him was covered with hair. Francine imagined that this was how it felt to be around Jesus. Not that Zech was Jesus, nor she his disciple, but he exuded that kind of spiritual ease that she imagined must have existed in the first century. And of course, every depiction of Jesus Francine had ever seen showed him with long hair and beard so there was that to consider.

Francine chuckled to herself.

"Share the laugh?" Zechariah said. His eyes never leaving the cutting board where he was chopping something that looked like a long, hairy purple twig.

It was Francine's turn not to respond.

"I'm thinking of shifting my focus to perceptions of women's roles in the most populated ethnic groups in Ghana."

One of Zech's eyebrows raised.

"What?!" Francine asked.

"Both your conscious mind and subconscious loves controversy."

Francine rolled her eyes.

"Not true. It's just that this whole situation has got me thinking. If that were a man in the video, would there be such outrage? Would I have lost the Fellowship? Not just here but in the States, too. The double standard is real. Maybe I'll include some kind of comparisons across the diaspora."

Zech shook his head. Francine would figure it out, he was certain of that. Her brainstorming process was just much more frenetic than his.

"So tell me about your meeting," he asked.

"What meeting?" Francine said and smiled.

"Coy doesn't look natural on you."

Francine laughed.

"And yet I play it so well."

Zech shook his head again. The woman was something.

Francine shared with him some of the details of the meeting, mostly because she figured he already knew them and was just seeing what she would leave out. At this point, she didn't really think it would matter much either way, especially since Zechariah had somehow found himself in her files.

"How were you able to get them to let Joseph continue to drive for me?"

"Who said I did?"

"They said it."

Zech took the purple root he'd meticulously chopped into tiny quarter-inch pieces and funneled them into a glass jar.

"Hmmm."

Francine didn't bother to press him anymore.

"Oh, but there was this one woman there, I had no idea who she was. They called her Midim."

Zechariah looked up from the bottle. His chestnut-colored eyes widened for the first time since Francine had met him. He let the surprise linger on his face a few moments then went back to his more somber demeanor.

"Tell me about her," he said.

"There's not much to tell," Francine said. "She had reddish auburn dyed hair. Pressed and curled and …"

Zech lifted and waved his hand, cutting her off mid-sentence, "The NanaBenz."

"Nana-who?"

Zech pointed to Francine's cell phone, "Look them up."

Francine Googled "The NanaBenz" and began reading.

It seems as though she and Ursula had correctly guessed that Midim was one of the owners of the largest textile manufacturing company in the region. What they didn't know was that Midim was a part of the powerful collective called NanaBenz, a group of African businesswomen who'd built empires and made billions in the markets—all under the noses of multinational companies who believed themselves to be the most influential.

"Woah."

Zechariah smirked, "Woah is right."

Francine was silent for a few a minutes as she processed the depths of the network and how royally she'd jacked up her opportunity. Then she remembered another question she had.

"You know, they also mentioned someone named LaVaughn. About ruining her reputation and making her look bad. I've done a lot of research on the women that I know of in this group, but there is no one connected to them named LaVaughn."

Zechariah smiled again. For the first time, it occurred to her how perfect his teeth were—model straight and so white they seemed translucent when the light touched his smile in just the right way.

"Are you sure about that?" Zech turned on the stove again and put on a pot of water.

"Of course I'm sure. LaVaughn is kind of a hard name to miss."

"I suppose. Unless it happens to be a middle name. Like, say, Michelle LaVaughn Robinson …"

"… OBAMA?!" Francine finished his sentence with a shriek.

Zech nodded.

Ursula was right!

Suddenly, the shame returned like a hot-and-sticky noose around her neck. It was hard to breathe, hard to see. She'd blown her opportunity to connect with the most powerful black women in the world, including the First Lady of the United States. *So much for that dream of tea with her imaginary best friend forever, Mimi Obama.*

Shame told Francine that she'd squandered it all because she wasn't worthy of having it in the first place. It whispered in her heart that she'd never really be free of Garrison. *Isn't that why all of this happened? Me just wanting to let my hair down and not think about how badly that man hurt me. He's probably back in Patrice's family's good graces, enjoying box seats at Lincoln Center or checking out the latest MOMA exhibit, and I'm 13,000 miles away trying to find another place to live and salvage my career.*

When Francine's mind returned to the present, a hot steaming cup of "crazy tea," as she called it, was sitting in front of her and Zechariah was gone. A deep moan, reminiscent of the old Negro spirituals sung by deacons in an old African American Baptist church was followed by light humming. It filled the house.

***

After downing the tea, Francine followed the melody of Zech's humming back into the greenhouse. She had to admit that she was fascinated by his work. The medicinal use of herbs was not beyond the scope of her own study of culture, particularly within vibrant indigenous origins. It was the science of it that tripped her up.

Zech was standing in the fourth aisle of the greenhouse looking at the leaves of a plant through a magnifying glass.

"So what are you working on?"

Zech looked around. "Where would you like me to begin?"

Francine picked up a paper that sat on one of the tables that marked the end of row.

> *The Susu people inhabit parts of West African, including Sierra Leone and Guinea. They are the descendants of the Mali Empire. The Susu are mostly farmers with the primary crops being rice and millet. They also grow mangoes, pineapples, and coconuts. The women in this ethnic group are often known for their ability to heal both physical and mental ailments using rare herbs only found on the coast.*

"So tell me about this? I thought susu was the money network. What does this have to do with your work?"

Zechariah shrugged, "Not *that* susu."

Francine was frustrated. She was over trying to make Zech talk. She had enough on her mind without trying pry into the mysterious work of Dr. Zechariah Johns.

"Okay then, well I'm going to call Joseph."

"It's the central focus of the work," he said in his quiet, rumbling voice.

Francine was confused. “What?”

Zech put down his magnifying glass and walked up the aisle toward Francine. “What you just read is one part of the driving purpose of my latest inquiry.”

Francine was officially fascinated. “What inquiry?”

Zech stared at Francine for a moment. Her interest seemed real. Her eyes twinkled with curiosity.

“Well … I’ve found evidence that in the coastal areas of Sierra Leone where the Susu ethnic group predominately lives, there is a very rare strain of lavender, that functions kind of like a truth serum.”

“A truth serum? You mean, as in *Mission Impossible*, inject Tom Cruise once and he’ll tell the bad guys the bomb activation code, truth serum?”

Zechariah laughed loudly and heartily. It was the first time he’d ever heard anyone describe his work that way.

“Well, not quite. But that would be good too.” He laughed more and walked down the next aisle. Francine followed him.

“No, this, I believe, was used as early as the 16th century as more of a clarifying agent. If taken in small doses, a person became deeply and completely aware of himself, inside and out. He became clear about what he wanted and why he wanted it.”

“Ohhh, so this herb susus you into self-awareness. It’s like drinking a shot glass of self-knowledge. Well, that’s new. Soon people will be walking around saying, ‘Don’t get susued!’ or “Don’t make me susu you!’”

Zech shook his head and chuckled, “Really, Francine?” But then, his voice quickly turned serious.

“If you are going to do well, you had better take the time to take some of these treasured aspects of the various cultures here seriously. It is the very least expected of you. When you don’t, it is a sign of *your* disrespect, your American ugliness. Inroads for your research will shut down quickly.”

“Duly noted—Ethnography aka Humanity 101,” she said. “You’re right. I know better.”

Francine really did know better but appreciated Zech calling her on the lapse. This is why she was here, to live all of the things she studied about all of those years. This was the kind of challenge she welcomed. She felt humbled and began to redirect her energies. She needed to get serious about herself again, get reacquainted with her best self.

"That said, yes, in a small way you are correct. I think self-awareness is severely lacking nowadays. I guess you can say that both scientifically and metaphorically, I'm in search of susu for myself and the rest of the world."

Francine smiled. The first real smile she'd given since her infamous night on the town. She suspected it was because, in her own way, she also needed some susu in her life.

13

Francine ended up spending the next several days at Zech's place. She understood why he lived 90 kilometers, as the locals said, out of the city. The farm was alive with sights and sounds but mostly scents. At night, they sat out on the porch stargazing, Zech from an old but sturdy rocking chair, Francine from the hammock that had become her cradle, about 5 feet away. They'd talk for an hour or two about something or nothing. If the lantern was not lit, it took a while for their eyes to adjust to the pitch black of a night illuminated only by the moon and stars—a truly majestic sight. It was hard for Francine to believe it could get that dark out. Afterward, they'd go inside and end up in the kitchen over a pot of tea and talk some more.

Zech was a great listener. Francine was learning that a pause in a conversation did not have to be dramatic. Contemplation did not have to be reserved for some vague time after a dialogue. It could be of value in the present. During the day, Francine usually had a moment of shame and tears, recalling the train wreck she had caused. This would be followed by some time of reflection. Then, typically she continued with a bit of writing. She'd begun organizing and strategizing her recovery and needed the quiet of the empty house. Zech usually returned from his lab around 3 p.m. each day, clad in lightweight overalls cut at the shins, wiping his brow with a small worn towel he kept tucked in his back pocket. Wearing an out of shape UCLA t-shirt or tank top and old shoes or sneakers, his locks were wrapped up into a knot at the nape of his neck.

Some days Francine would ride the four kilometers with him to the merchant center where he could collect or post mail at a place that served as an internet café, market, and transportation depot. People could take a minibus, a motorcycle taxi, or hire a private car for errands or longer trips. *Mayberry-esque*, she thought.

Sometimes they would take the truck, an old pick up. Usually, they took the motorcycle, which was better equipped to pass the bumpy parts of the unpaved roads where Zech lived. He wasn't entirely sure she was up for the ride, but Francine was in such despair, it didn't even occur to her to be wary. Zech knew the roads very well. She held on tight and pressed the side of her face to the empty canvas backpack he wore in order to avoid the loose pebbles and dust that rose up on the less traveled sections of the ride. No one wore helmets, which freaked her out.

Once at the market, Zech would check for any mail or messages, exchange greetings and pleasantries mostly in English. Then, they'd select vegetables and a fresh yard bird dressed on the premises. He took a few minutes to read and return email (Francine was still avoiding hers), and they would be on their way. On the return trip, she wore the backpack filled with the purchases and mail and held on to Zech for dear life. This time, her cheek pressed against his sweaty shirt. His scent was a pungent mix of sweat, dirt, and plant life.

While he showered, she would set the table and insist on acting as sous chef to dinner. Then, she'd wash dishes and sweep up after. It was the least she could do. He said she could stay as long as she'd like and come back anytime. The house was seldom locked as the next place was a good mile away. He kept the key on the hammock hook.

Francine spent many of her mornings following Zech around the grounds of the farm, as he narrated his daily operations of tending the greenhouse and outdoor plant beds. He described what each area meant to his research, the marketplace, and his personal uses. Francine listened at times but mostly caught only bits and pieces, noting only the scents of the plants. Walking had always taken her mind to the things she tucked away in her subconscious. It didn't take Zech long to sense that Francine needed the walks more than the talks, and so he learned to leave her with her thoughts for most of the morning routine.

What Francine took from the routine was just what she needed. Zech's routine wasn't rote because the herbs were dynamic living things with different needs with each season. Many had properties which varied depending on the conditions: interaction with other herbs, stimuli, light, and temperature, etc. Some worked well together, others thrived best only amongst their own. Some could be manipulated, others not so much. Some were extremely potent, others fairly innocuous. Francine kept going on the walks because the properties of the herbs seemed awfully similar to her life. As Zech took verbal inventory in the care and nurturing of his plants, she did so with her past, her work, The Search, the Sherman, Garrison, the DIP room—all to reground the self she had let slip. As Zech's watering reconstituted plants that had gone limp, the symbolism in it all led Francine on an inventory of her emotional, intellectual, and spiritual self. She continued the walks because the relationship she observed between Zech and his herbs was respectfully interdependent: In some ways they needed each other, in some ways they didn't. Both had the power to soothe or destroy the other. Zech's ever-present awareness of that reality impressed Francine as necessary in uprighting the capsized search for fulfillment in her own pursuits. Before she even got started, her little performance had blasted to pieces the solid foundation lain for her as a Search fellow.

She was very much cast out.

Francine recalled the words in the follow-up letter sent by TCC: *The place we set for you has been taken up. The Queen Mothers who were to present you as an honored guest among their people, will do so no longer. You, our guest, have brought a shame that cannot be tolerated. Perhaps you should begin at the universities in the city. In the city, they tend to be more laissez-faire about this kind of thing.*

****

Joseph called Francine to let her know he would arrive at her hotel in a few minutes to move her things. It was time.

She had spent three weeks at Zech's—a much-needed retreat to reboot the messy start of her journey. After her meeting with the TCC, Zech had arranged for Joseph to collect her things from the ambassador housing and reserve her room at Mr. Addo's hotel. The hotel was in a suburb just outside of Accra. It was a far cry from the diplomat housing of modern mansions on manicured, tropical tree-lined streets and nearby trendy restaurants. Yet, it held a charm and grit Francine could appreciate. The area had several churches that broadcasted their services on loudspeakers each morning. It also had a mosque and countless homeowners who sold dry goods and other items in pop-up style shops. On the main street was a police station, radio station, SIM card kiosks, Pakistani-owned carryout restaurants, and clothing stores displaying familiar items sold by the street vendors back in Philly. After having a modest breakfast of tea, eggs, and bread in the open-air dining room, Joseph collected her most mornings around 10. They spent the day visiting the historic sites and other must-see attractions around Accra, with a day trip here and there up to tour the slave castle museums of Cape Coast or the weaving demonstrations and Ashanti cultural centers in Kumasi. She had read so much and seen so many documentaries about the official history, it hardly seemed new. Still, it meant something to see, touch, and smell it for herself.

Her trip to the Kwame Nkrumah museum was bittersweet. She had planned to spend a good time with their curators as a Search fellow. Oh well … Ironically, Francine learned the most from the time they spent in traffic. You could buy anything you could imagine along a roadside, from vendors in the middle of the streets or at the tolls rudimentarily set up along roads between regions, towns, etc.

There were some comforts of home as well. They visited the local malls, where she could patronize designer fabric boutiques as one would a designer clothing store. Francine was beginning to understand that the clothing market in Ghana was about the quality and design of the fabric more so than the items of clothing made from them. It seemed terribly involved and fascinating. They also visited huge quasi-open markets where shoppers could purchase everything from plumbing fixtures and accessories for the home to everyday essentials like ready-to-wear clothes, baby items, soap, cell phones, etc. The fabric area was most impressive and a market unto itself. Francine made a note to return there before she visited the dressmaker again and to send some samples to her mother to stock up for their West African clients. At the market, Joseph would park and escort her through the labyrinth of stores, booths, tables, and even blankets set up to display merchandise for sale. Women wrapped their heads, some with a small platform on top to help steady bags or baskets they carried expertly on their heads. Babies rested comfortably wrapped on the mothers' backs, little legs dangling from the wraps. This appeared to serve several purposes: keeping the mothers' arms free to carry more things, safeguarding the babies from some of the congestion of the crowds, and allowing the mothers who were working to keep the babies from being underfoot as they took care of their customers.

Francine was exhausted by the end of the day and was usually extracting the last drop of water from the small square bags of water she bought daily in traffic. After a shower, she would go up to the outdoor terrace for dinner. The evening cook had a far better disposition than the morning cook who dragged her feet around the breakfast room and overcharged her for her breakfast every other day. As the day cooled off, Francine ordered her meal of chicken with rice, grilled vegetables, and a cup of tea. She was typically one of only a few guests who took dinner on the terrace, but for her, it was incredibly relaxing. She enjoyed the warm breeze, the view overlooking the busy neighborhood, and the smell of burning trash. She would miss it.

Like clockwork, Joseph knocked on her door to carry her bags to the car.

"Are you ready, mum?" he asked.

"Yes, Joseph, I am ready."

Francine had grown attached to Joseph. He was an excellent guide and a great companion for her recent explorations. At her insistence, he had accompanied her into the museums and restaurants for lunch. At *his* insistence, he accompanied her to the markets and malls to help her bargain for fair prices. He had even introduced her to the supplier in the fabric market, Mr. Mawuli, who would select mourning cloths for various regions and ethnic groups that she would detail and send home to her parents. Francine wondered if Mr. Mawuli knew Midim.

Before she'd left his farm, Zech had made arrangements for her to stay in a house in what he only called a "good neighborhood." The home came with a live-in cook whose services were covered in the rent. Joseph could continue to drive for a good price. Zech had paid installments for the first three months. The Sherman would comfortably afford her the remaining months. He had a friend, Adjowa, who lived across the street who would help her with any other adjustments.

Francine could not tell how far they had traveled due to the time spent in traffic en route. When they arrived, Joseph helped her with her bags, then took her over to Adjowa's for introductions. The houses were gated by brick or iron. Adjowa's was a tasteful combination. Inside the gate was a nicely maintained lawn, with a slate walking path and colorful flowers along the borders. Two well-fed rabbits chased each other playfully. Joseph knocked on a side door shaded by 9-foot shrubs. It looked as if someone had been enjoying a moment or more of leisure. There was small table and chair just beyond the shrubs. On the tabletop were a magazine, cell phone, and remnants of breakfast. The housekeeper, a polite young woman, informed them that Adjowa was traveling but was expected within the week.

Francine used the time to unpack, unwind, and plug back in. Joseph walked her around the four-block radius to orient her to the neighborhood. She logged on to her computer to check email. The message she was waiting for had arrived from Accra Metropolitan University:

Welcome, Professor Francine Carty:

We are pleased to accommodate a Sherman Fellow. Professors Able Gadzekpo and Amina Wellbeck are well traveled in the States and suited to orient you to our University, facilitating resources for your research. They have made themselves available to greet you this week, Wednesday 28 June @ 11:00 over lunch. You will meet at the Nkrumah-DuBois Conference Room.

Please confirm your receipt of this message via email.

Kind Regards,
Chancellor Kofi G. Amevo

"Hallelujah! Thank you, Jesus!" Francine shouted.

Though still far in the distance, she could see the light.

Francine confirmed immediately and busied herself preparing for the meeting the next week. In the meantime, she began to read through the 500-page tome of articles she compiled for herself during her weeks at Zech's.

Francine spent the next few days poring over the essays and articles by women scholars and activists from around the entire continent on the issue of oppression—economic, political, social, and sexual. The work was affirming, infuriating, and inspiring. More than a few of the readings referenced Mariama Ba's *So Long a Letter*, so she made a note to borrow a copy from the university and read it immediately. So much of what she read captured Francine's interest, but she needed to refine a focus. What ended up keeping her up at night was the social oppression. It was, after all, where she found herself in the moment. According to the literature, the consequences of moral failings proved far more difficult matters for women who come from traditional, socially conservative, collectivist communities. Francine was already an outsider, so she had only herself to contend with. The articles she read documented repercussions that left emotional, psychological, and even physical scars on women, all sanctioned by pride in family and community.

Francine came up for air only to eat, have some of the tea Zech sent back with her, and take potty breaks and showers. Joseph called to check on her.

"Mum, you have not called. Zech has asked me to inquire," he said.

"Thank you, Joseph. I am well. Just working very hard. And yes, I am eating well."

She knew he would ask. Francine was glad he called, because she had completely forgotten to make arrangements with him to drive her to the meeting.

"Sure, Mum. Please call if you need me before then." He seemed relieved his services were still needed.

She used the interruption to take a full break. She called home.

"Child, I was about to come over there and look for you! We called the number you gave us, and they said you weren't there anymore, no details or anything. I finally sent for Robbi to send some of her people to find you," her mom spilled a mix of joy, exasperation, and relief.

"Hi Mommy," was all Francine could muster. *Damn!* She almost said aloud. Now that Robbi was on her scent, her family would have to know of the catastrophe sooner than she was prepared to explain. She hadn't bothered to call Robbi after everything went down even though she'd initially planned to. She figured this was one strategy she needed to come up with on her own.

"Don't 'hi mommy' me, girl. What is going on over there? You had us scared half to death!" she went on.

To her own surprise, Francine told her mom the full truth. She heaved and cried the whole time, but she poured it all.

"Oh, baby," her mom sighed. Repeatedly.

"Your father just came home, so email Robbi your new number." Gwendolyn limited email communications to business. With personal matters, she was strictly old school. It was one of the ways she insisted on practicing discretion.

"I love you. Take *care* of yourself. You're too far from home, and as good as he's been to you, you don't know that Zechariah. Who are his people in America? Do we know them? Here comes your father. You want to talk or just tell him you called?"

"Just tell him I called. I'll call back this weekend," Francine sniffed. "I'm sorry and I'll stay in touch from now on, Mommy. I promise. Bye."

"Send Robbi your new address, too, and look for a letter from me soon! Bye baby," her mom whispered rapidly.

"Call us Sunday night if you can."

Francine was tired of crying, but she knew she was hardly finished and that she needed the purge.

***

The meeting and lunch with her new colleagues went well. Thankfully, their reception of her reflected no knowledge of her debacle at the BR. They were supportive of her research agenda and would connect her to the right people to ensure her time there was productive.

A week later, a letter arrived for Francine. It was from her mother.

My Dearest Francine,

It nearly broke my heart to learn what has happened to you there. I hope you can forgive us for leaving you adrift. Pride can both buoy and suffocate. We only intended it to lift you girls. You should know that your father and I have required so much of you, in part, to compensate for failings in our own pasts; pasts we have shielded from you.

Suffice it to say, I have been there. Your dad and I agreed never to tell you, but now, I think we must.

As a child, my family was very poor. So many of the upper classes in Montserrat treated us with disdain because my mother took men to her bed to feed us. I ran away when her companions began looking to me to do the same. I was taken in by a woman who found me on the street almost starving. She cleaned me up, raised me as her own. I helped her earn money by taking in laundry, sewing, and keeping house for a wealthy family of undertakers on the island. Your father worked for the same wealthy family, helping his dad dig graves and doing odd jobs around the estate. We were just kids then and became fast friends. He looked out for me.

One day, he went with me to visit my mother. I wanted to talk her into doing hair for the undertakers. She was so good with hair. It could have changed everything for her. When we arrived, she was sitting in the kitchen drinking the concoction she always prepared to help her forget the men when they left—a brew of fruit, herbs, and whiskey. Sound familiar?

Well, that day, one of her regulars was there and very drunk. He grabbed me by the neck and threw me onto the floor. My mother just sat there, sipping and forgetting. This time your father, who was waiting outside, responded to my screams. Thank God he had that shovel. He hit the man on the head, and he fell limp. We tried everything to get him to come to, but ... well, we just didn't know what else to do. He never came to.

And ... neither did my mother.

We ran into town and told them someone was sick back at my mother's house. When we were sure someone was being sent, I went back to the house where I was staying and your dad went back to his family. But of course, that wasn't the end of it. On the island, people began to talk. They said I had killed my own mother and that I had put roots on your father to help me kill the man. We were just kids! People were so cruel.

In those days, the coroner didn't spend too much time figuring out how poor black people like us ended up dead so there weren't any charges. But we were made outcasts; we were condemned and alienated. We weren't welcome at the schoolhouse, and even the church didn't want anything to do with us. Thank God the family we worked for didn't care about that kind of thing. Folks there weren't afraid of the dead, so we fit in just fine at the undertakers. We watched every funeral service and prayed as the mourners prayed. Honestly, that was our church. We helped prepare obituaries to practice our reading, and paid close attention in order to learn whatever we could from the undertaker about any and everything: anatomy, physiology, and chemistry from body prep, social studies from planning services that had to cater to all classes of grieving people, math from sewing, showing, selling funeral packages.

Despite the shame, your father and I planned. Over the years, we learned every detail of the funeral business and saved every bit of money we earned to get out of there and make a life for ourselves. We came here three months after we married. It wasn't easy, starting from scratch, but being free from the stigma allowed us to reap the benefits of our hard work. That didn't mean that the scars weren't there. It was tough to let go of the idea that we hadn't done anything wrong. Yes, we wore those scars a long time. And baby, they're deep.

Just before we left, I finally got up the courage to ask Dr. Matthisen, the town doctor, how my mother died. That had been weighing on me because I wasn't sure what happened. I learned that she'd overdosed. She had put something extra in her brew that day. I guess she was just tired of it all. Plus, the man she was with, Mr. Eason, had a reputation for attacking women and alcohol abuse. She probably knew what was coming.

For years after that, I worked to perfect that recipe for the Carty "Burial" Brew Tea. I figured it's my way of remembering something good about my mother and helping people forget their grief, if only for a moment.

Here's the thing, my sweet girl. With the love of your father and good friends who have their own secrets and crosses to bear, I have learned to not allow the horrors of my past to define who I am.

Just because you were involved in something despicable, does not make you disposable.

I now regret that we didn't share these details with you girls earlier. We thought if we taught you to achieve your goals despite difficulties, you could make it in the world once we're gone. We neglected to teach you that happiness and fulfillment could exist distinct from your goals. I also fear we never made clear that your achievements, though we celebrate them, do not determine the degree of our love. We could never love you more or less than we ever have. Our love is unconditional. Always know this.

Read this note as often as you need to. I suggest keeping it in your Bible, try near Romans 8:1. Remember, as much as we love you, you must seek comfort with your Father in heaven.

We love you,
Mom & Dad

Francine went straight to the Bible she kept at her bedside and read the scripture through teary eyes: *"There is therefore no condemnation for those who are in Christ Jesus…"*

She inserted her mother's letter and released all of the pressure, grief, shame, and anxiety she had been carrying for years. She awakened in the middle of the night, feeling drained but empty in a good way. Her mother swore by the power of personal letters. Rereading the letter, Francine found herself interpreting everything about it—its writing, sealing, sending, traveling, arriving, opening, unfolding, and reading was an opportunity to declare intimacy, to document one's vulnerability and triumph over life's transgressions between hearts. She decided, in that moment, that she would find a way to use letter writing in some way in her research on social oppression and women. As she sat at the small writing desk, Francine decided she would begin with her own.

***

The very next evening, she spent several hours across the street at Adjowa's. They had become very friendly. Adjowa was only two or three years her senior and lived a lifestyle that extremely understated her wealth as a businesswoman. Francine affectionately called her Baby-Benz because of that. Over a pot of tea in Adjowa's kitchen, Francine read the letter she had written acknowledging the deep-seated feelings of inadequacy that had culminated in the episode in the DIP and the loss of the Search. Adjowa listened in silence, stirring her tea. When Francine finished, Adjowa gave her a long hug.

"Wait here," Adjowa said placing a roll of paper towels center table next to Francine.

She returned from the back room, pulling the young housekeeper by the hand. The girl looked frightened.

"Esi, sit down." Adjowa sat the girl down. You need to hear this.

"Francine, please. She needs to hear your letter. Esi will keep it private, eh?" The girl, curious but mostly obedient, agreed.

As Francine read her letter, tears streamed down Esi's face. Adjowa held her hand and insisted she listen to the entire letter. Esi, then told her story. She shared that she had come to live with Adjowa from her village because she had disgraced her family. As the most promising math and science student in the school, she was sent to a university overseas in the States. While there, she could not find work on campus, so in desperation, she took a job "cooking" in a meth lab to earn fast money and save time to focus on her studies. In her final year, the meth house was raided. She was deported and returned home in shackles. Her parents sent her to Adjowa.

"We did not raise you to 'cook'! Since you *want* to cook, we have made arrangements for you to do so. Do not show yourself here again," Esi recounted, with anguish, her parents' parting words to her.

Francine reeled. She returned to her house and spent all night pulling together excerpts from the essays and articles by West African women that spoke to the issue of redemption of women over social oppression. She wanted to be able to offer women healing words they could carry with them. The most powerful words would have to be from women from their own cultures.

Should it be a seminar, workshop, or something else, something more intimate?

Next she worked on the format. It needed to be reciprocal. There would be tea and, of course, brew for those who preferred it. There needed to be confidentiality and community.

Francine settled on the following:

- word of mouth only
- Six to seven women who delivered letters to Francine outlining interest in participating and the name of the woman who had referred her.
- Francine would contact the referrals with an invitation for the woman to join the next gathering.
- The gatherings would be hosted at Francine's or in the home of one of the participants
- Each participant should bring a covered dish; Francine would provide the tea, brew and her own dish.
- The gatherings would open with tea she brought back from Zech's farm, introductions and a confidentiality ritual.
- Francine would open the discussion with selected excerpts from African women's writings on social oppression, then begin with her own letter and watershed moment.
- The other participants would follow, and the women would support each in her embarking on the road to redemption.
- They would then dine and bond over burial brew or tea.

- They would close the meeting repeating the confidentiality ritual, which hours later, held far more weight and far less mistrust.
- In cases when people traveled long distances, Francine and Adjowa would accommodate them overnight. Joseph was on hand to drive participants home when needed.
- Finally, she would make a sign that read:

Comfort Conversations
featuring
Burial Brew

The first gathering was held at Adjowa's. In attendance were guests of Adjowa, Esi, Joseph, and Julia—one of Francine's colleagues from the university. Francine was nervous, but Adjowa, Esi, and Julia encouraged her from the kitchen and helped out by setting up the food and serving the drinks. Francine decided to offer the brew up front, which did its job of loosening the anxiety. She presented it as an old family recipe used to "soothe spiritual suffering and forget one's worries for a spell." The women laughed in recognition and held out their teacups. After four hours, the women had laughed, cried, hugged, fed their bodies and spirits with acceptance, inspirational words, and left feeling a bit lighter.

As Joseph left to drive two of the women home, Francine went outside to join Adjowa and Esi and to exhale.

"Francine, this is good work you have started here," Adjowa grasped her hands encouragingly. "From out here, it sounded as if they did not want to leave!"

"Yes! It was good, it was good!" Francine took a deep breath squeezing both of Adjowa's hands in return. She gestured for Esi to join them, and she thanked them both as the women held hands. Esi withdrew first and retreated briskly into the house.

Francine worried that Esi sharing her "fall" from grace had reopened the wound.

"I'm not sure that's it, Francine. Something's been disturbing her for the two years she's been here. She left something in the States. I don't know if it's a lover or what. Maybe it's just *what she could have made of herself*, but I think it's something else. I've asked her, but she's silent.

"Can't she go to school here?"

"I've offered to help her, but she refuses. Says she doesn't want to disappoint anyone again—that she must do it on her own. Almost every night, she's on the computer, looking at that university she left. That road is closed. She can't go back to the States. She'll be arrested as a felon!"

Francine agreed.

"Leave it for her to figure out. You, my friend have work to do. I can see you'll have women from all over knocking on your door. You restrict these meetings to Fridays, eh?" Adjowa advised.

Francine considered Adjowa's words. "That's actually a good problem to have. But, I see your point. It's exhausting. Thank you again. For everything!"

She squeezed Adjowa's hand once more before heading toward the gate leading to the street.

Francine took a quick shower and prepared herself for bed. She would write up her notes from the meeting in the morning. But first she would call her mother. And Zech.

***

Over the next few months, Francine held Comfort Conversations in her home and the homes of participants. Throughout the semester, women faculty hosted her in facilitating sessions on campuses around the country, even as she continued the conversations in private homes on weekends. The gatherings often started as a juxtaposition of mourning and promise. Francine began with her own letter. In it she read aloud to the women her feelings of inadequacy, the binds of pride and expectation, her self-valuation related to romantic relationships, and finally she recounted in vivid detail the transgression that led to her fall from grace and the remaining uncertainty of how it would impact her academic career upon her return to the States. Drawing on her teaching materials on transgenerational trauma, she contextualized her mother's revelation and it's power to help her recover her power.

The women, who came from varied ages, stations in life, religion, and ethnicities, appreciated her openness and affirmed and challenged the examples Francine used to guide the discussion from the scholarship she'd read on the social oppression of West African women. Participants were invited to share letters they'd written in preparation for the intimate exchange. There were lots of tears, hugs, some singing, revelation, more affirmation, a feast, and, of course, tea.

The months flew by. Robbi's time in Botswana was not the cakewalk she expected, so she wasn't as available as expected but checked in at critical moments. Francine spent time at Zech's place fleshing out her plans as her work progressed as well as learning to select herbs for tea. As she found her legs, his place became her refuge. Zech was shoulder-deep in his research. In contrast to his strict work and healthy dietary discipline, his appearance was now full-on wolf man—just overalls and wily hair. His voice had become his only recognizable feature. *How did he tolerate all that hair in 80-degree weather?* In direct proportion, Francine had become obsessed with the intricate flat twist styles her hair-braider made for her. Her hair was growing like weeds, and she didn't have the time to maintain a full-grown twist out fro. So every few weeks, she spent hours taking out, washing, then having her hair braided.

Zech loved to comment on the elaborate braided styles she had begun to wear. Francine had been truly surprised to observe that many of the women she met used hair relaxers or long weaves. Part of her nonverbal lexicon was the celebration of black women's natural aesthetic, so she *kept* her hair looking flawless in styles that she and her braid stylist came up with. It was important for her that during the intimate conversations she had with women, she demonstrated an appreciation of her natural self. But she never commented on the women's choices of weaves and relaxers for fear they would see her as judging them. She recognized and understood all too well, the pressures black women faced regarding their God-given tresses.

After determining who brought which rice dish or stew, her hair was often an icebreaker at the meetings, particularly among the older women who recalled how hair braiding was once a beloved traditional art form.

Another point of conversation from the women was Francine's physical transformation. Francine had begun wearing wrap skirts and dresses in beautiful fabrics that hugged hips that were rounding out from the flavorful rice and beans (and grilled vegetables) she enjoyed almost daily. The women often commented on how easily she could find a husband with her good child-bearing hips and smooth skin. Francine was so preoccupied with her work, she hadn't even noticed the lack of effort required to properly maintain her skin—a regular regimen of hers back home. She had almost blindly followed Adjowa's recommendations for personal care products when hers ran out. A true friend of Zech's, everything Adjowa suggested—from head to toe—was homemade by one of the women who came to the first meeting.

During her travels to the farm, Francine and Zech continued the tradition of sharing dinner, then talking, listening, drinking tea, and stargazing from his front porch. She teased him about becoming a voice in the wilderness, *literally*. He chuckled and in turn addressed her as the beans and rice bride. It was the perfect retreat.

In the last few months, Zech had begun traveling up and down the coast for his own research, so wasn't always there. Still, the farm had become her second home. She mastered riding the motorbike and even learned the intricacies of his research now that she was on firm footing with her own agenda. Their friendship became a kinship. For Francine, he was less the sage and more the confidante and sounding board for her next steps. Zech had become a great supporter. When he couldn't be there, he'd leave tea recipes for her to try for her meetings and a supply for her personal medicinal use—

the latter being a critical factor in her no longer needing her fibro meds and not having had a flare in months.

As her Sherman fellowship came to an end, a whirlwind of celebrations marked her preparation to return to the States. The University held a wonderful reception in her honor, a group of women in the community held a party for her, and Adjowa, to whom she had grown as close as a sister, held a feast in her home where family, neighbors, Judith the dressmaker, her hair-braider, and Joseph celebrated her. Zech, who was in Sierra Leone at the time, surprised her with a phone call wishing her a heartfelt farewell. The goodbye call from Zech was the fait accompli that brought her to tears. He had truly witnessed her come full circle.

They all gave her notes sharing their sentiments about their time with her. Esi busied herself keeping the food prepped. The day before, she had come to Francine's to say goodbye, then ran back across the street sobbing.

***

Settling into her first class seat, Francine reflected on how her life had changed since her last intercontinental flight. With an invitation in hand from the Sherman Fellowship, she was slated to give the luncheon keynote at the annual Sherman Scholars dinner. News of her work and its impact in academia and the community had caught the attention of the Sherman's government sponsors. She received the invitation a month before and had been working on her talk.

She couldn't help but to feel like being back in Philadelphia was like returning to the scene of the crime. It was a strange sensation for sure. She knew she would spend the week there. She would deliver her presentation, catch up with Ursula, drop by the bar, and most definitely, reach out to Byron to thank him personally for the quick save. She was undecided whether she'd stop in to see Roseline or Mrs. Fortley. Despite the success of her research, the TCC and U.S. contingent of The Search seemed to have washed their hands of Dr. Francine M. Carty. Francine contemplated letting sleeping dogs lie but a huge part of her wanted to reach out and offer a formal apology, at least once she was settled.

Until then, she planned to go home to Maryland and conduct a job search from there. She was looking forward to spending quality time with her parents and talking out her parents' past with them to better understand the connection to her own pain and determine its impact on her work.

Francine slept the entire flight. She hadn't realized how hard she had worked due to how much the work inspired her. Upon waking an hour before the aircraft began its descent, she had to laugh recalling meeting Zechariah. She wished she had seen more of him in her last few months. She'd eventually stopped going to the farm when he was out of town because it just wasn't the same when he wasn't there. It was like coming home to see family, but no one being home. The things were familiar but the actual family was absent. She knew they would be lifelong friends. He had become a part of her story and she of his.

It was so refreshing to have a true friendship with a man, regardless of age or romance—a genuine appreciation of each other's humanity, warts and all. The last time she saw him, she admonished him for letting his locs and beard grow out of control. He shared with her that he only had them groomed professionally when he traveled for presentations—other than that, the lack of attention to them was indicative of his immersion in his work.

"I'm getting close, you know. The next time you see me, my head and face could be shaved!" he said. "I'm close to finding my susu."

They laughed and raised their teacups. She couldn't imagine him without hair or not spending hours in his greenhouse. His head was a wily mass of grey and black hair, with a perfect enchanting smile that betrayed his otherwise gentle Grizzly Adams look. She wasn't sure she would recognize anything but his smile upon seeing him clean-shaven. *He must have been a lady killer in his day*, she often thought.

Before Francine knew it, Ursula was running toward her as she emerged from the last security exit of Philadelphia International Airport. Shrieking, the old friends embraced and caught up at the now *tenured* Associate Professor Ursula St. James' home—aka Frankie's old place. After showers and dinner, Ursula got serious.

"Uh-oh, what's wrong?" Frankie said, still on her home-at-last high.

"Things were going so well for you I didn't want to tell you," Ursula said.

Francine braced herself, "Urs, you're scaring me."

Ursula shared that the video of her, despite Byron's intervention, had managed to circulate just a bit. She had heard from a friend who was on a Sherman in South America that the other scholars were abuzz about the selection of the now infamous luncheon keynote.

Frankie smiled a sad resolute smile, "I was concerned about this. Now that it has come to pass, it confirms my decision to make it part of my presentation. A redemption story, if you will."

This brought Ursula to tears. The friends embraced in their pajamas and slippers.

"I am so proud of you," Ursula said.

Changing the tone completely, Ursula said, "Now. Can you do my hair like yours?" The sister friends burst into laughter and shared a bottle of Riesling for old times sake.

Frankie would spend the next 48 hours preparing to face the music, this time on *her* terms.

14

"*Heeeeey, baaaaby. One by one, y'all come and get these cherries. You know you want to. 'Who will be my boy toy, my boy toy.'*"

Francine stared out at the audience. Her face remained stoic even as her heart beat wildly. The facial expressions ran the gamut. Mouths agape in shock. Stunned embarrassment. Wrinkled brows. She'd expected it all. She was prepared for it all. When the 15-second excerpt of the video stopped, she allowed the silence to linger. She wanted them to sit with the discomfort. Wrestle with it. Be forced to reconcile their perceptions of the poised woman standing before them with the expertly tailored suit, lined with elaborate African fabric and braids pulled back in a neat professional bun, with the woman in the video, eyes and hair wild, white panties askew, streaks of whipped cream running down her torso.

"For most of you, this video is appalling. Maybe even all of you. After this luncheon, you might say to your colleagues, 'There is no place for that in our "scholarly" environment. You might even question my sanity, because surely she ..." Francine used the digital pointer to aim at her own face on the screen, "... has committed career suicide."

Nervous chuckles filled the air.

"And perhaps you're right. But I submit that even more telling is what some of you won't necessarily say aloud. 'Well, I can't say I'm surprised. Most of them are like that.' Or, 'See? And they wonder why they end up raped or assaulted.' Or, 'She should never be able to teach again. She is a horrible example.' *These* thoughts are the most telling, not because there is any truth to them—there isn't. They are revealing in that they are indicative of a larger more insidious issue that has taken root ..."

Francine smiled at the metaphor as an image of Zech flashed in her mind.

"... in many cultures around the world, including our own."

Francine nodded at the audio-visual technician who replaced the still image from the last frame of her video with the first slide in her PowerPoint presentation.

"I opened my presentation with this video because, frankly, this one solitary moment, this incredibly poor choice, exacerbated by an unintended interaction between prescription meds and alcohol, represents both an end and beginning in my life. The end because it was the absolute last time I allowed the entirety of who I am—as a scholar, an educator, a woman—to be defined by a single moment, by one decision. The beginning because, well, it was also the beginning of my greatest work thus far.

"I went to West Africa initially to explore the deliberate and varied cultural presentations of the legacy of the first post-colonial Ghanaian president, Kwame Nkrumah—purveyor of the Ghana black star that signifies the freedom and independence struggle of a nation that wrested itself from an oppressive hold. But it took this awful humiliation and the heart-wrenching losses that came along with it to bring me to an epiphany. In the words of someone very dear to me, I learned to accept that I was not disposable just because I'd done something despicable.

"So ... my work became bigger, more nuanced than cultural interpretation and collective memory could have ever been for me. I realized that there was another deliberate and varied cultural presentation right in front of me that needed to be investigated. A cultural legacy different from any I'd ever studied, yet deeply familiar. I had a chance to observe, study, and record the emotional, psychological, and dare I say, spiritual colonization of women who were living with the stigma of social oppression. Women halfway around the world who looked just like me."

Francine paused to allow the weight of her words to settle on the now fully engaged audience.

"Today, I'm going to present to you just a few of my findings from my upcoming paper, formally titled, "Notes to Self: How Creative Expression and Storytelling Link Women in Communities that Perpetuate Social Oppression."

***

Francine shut it down.

The completion of her 30-minute presentation was met with whooping that would make Arsenio Hall proud. The standing ovation lasted a few minutes, but what humbled Francine the most were the many women in the room—of every ethnicity, religion, young and old—who were visibly holding back tears, their eyes were wells waiting to overflow. Not only had she diffused her own scandal, she'd taken back her life and redefined both herself and her work. West Africa, though it had been a place where her hardest lesson was learned, had also brought out of her an authenticity, a natural confidence and grace that had been hidden for way too long under the sediment of her insecurities. Well, West Africa and a certain bearded man. Francine couldn't wait to write Zech and thank him for all he'd done. Like the susu plant he searched for, she'd finally found that strain of self-awareness that was rare and prized. And she planned to hold onto it forever.

After the luncheon, Francine was invited to a private cocktail reception to be attended by the full board of the Sherman Fellowship, as well as program sponsors, university administrators, and government officials. The flash of fear that rose up in her as she considered what they all might think of her after seeing the video was quickly dashed when everyone in the room practically lined up to shake her hand. She'd even had an exciting conversation with the Dean of Women's Studies at the University of Virginia who'd all but implied that there was a place for her there, if she was interested.

If I'm interested? Francine laughed to herself as she thought about how, only a year ago, she was a professor/phone sex operator/bartender who was practically begging for a full-time teaching position.

Funny how things change.

Francine turned to grab one of the shrimp cocktail hors d'oeuvres from a tray held by a tall, thin server with blond hair and blank eyes. Just as she put the decadent crustacean in her mouth, she nearly choked as her eyes met his.

Garrison.

Aaaand I guess some things don't.

Garrison grinned at her as he walked toward his former lover. But before he could get to her, Dr. Bronson, the Sherman Fellowship coordinator called Francine over to meet members of the board who were not seated on the dais during the luncheon. Francine was glad for the save as her mind had suddenly scattered and she needed time to regroup from the shock of seeing Garrison so soon after her return.

Francine followed the balding Dr. Bronson over to the other side of the large ballroom where two women stood to greet her. Francine was floored.

God, you are freaking hilarious!

"Dr. Carty, I'd like you to meet two of our most honorable trustees, Mrs. Isola Fortley of Philadelphia and Mrs. Stephanie Lashley of New York."

Francine shook the women's hands as though she'd never met them, following their lead. Mrs. Lashley kept her mouth contorted in the same grimace she wore when Francine sat in front of The Search committee all those months ago. Mrs. Fortley however, allowed her hand to linger slightly longer than was common. Francine didn't miss the twinkle in the old woman's eyes.

"It is my pleasure to meet such a brilliant young woman. You know I love a good redemption story, and yours dear, well yours is one of the best."

Unbelievable, Francine thought as she later walked back to the elevator that would take her to the suite she was booked in for the weekend, courtesy of The Sherman Fellowship. *Or was it The Search? They were on the board all along. They had my back all along.*

Francine shook her head at the turn of events. Walking on autopilot, she didn't see the man with broad shoulders, narrow waist, and bronze skin standing right in front of her until it was too late.

"Excuse …" Francine narrowly missed bumping into him.

"Me. Excuse me," Garrison said.

Francine felt the familiar pull of her body. *Noooooooooo.*

"Hey," Francine said. That's all she really had in the moment.

"Hey yourself," Garrison smiled. His dimples emerged, taunting her.

"That was an amazing keynote."

"Thanks."

"I mean, I don't know about the video part, but …"

Francine held up her hand as if to say, "*Don't even go there.*"

Garrison heeded her silent request.

"Listen, can we talk?" Garrison said.

"I thought that's what we were doing."

"No, I mean … alone."

Francine looked around. The last vestiges of people from the cocktail party were leaving.

"Let's have a drink. I had a bottle of vino sent to your room when I heard you would be here," he said, a little too eagerly. "Oh wait, did you …"

He was going to ask her about her meds. She wasn't going to bother to tell him that she wasn't on them anymore. That her friend, Zechariah, had given her a wonderful combination of herbs that worked better than the narcotics ever did. Nope, she wouldn't tell him. It wasn't any of his business.

Anymore.

"Listen, I have a dinner meeting and an early morning tomorrow," she said.

Garrison reached out and touched Francine's arm. The charge that shot through her body startled her.

"Please?"

Francine knew this day was coming. She just didn't know it would be so soon. She and Garrison did need to talk. They needed to clear the air, if for no other reason than to set each other free from the burden of "what might have been." Francine nodded, and they both turned and walked the remaining 10 steps to the elevator.

When the doors opened, another man stood in the left corner of the space. He was strikingly handsome in an expertly tailored suit reminiscent of styles she'd seen in Ghana. Garrison and Francine got on and stood on the right. As Garrison deftly slipped Francine's keycard from her hand and slid it into the VIP slot, Francine took a peek at the man and found him staring at her. His hair was cut close in a perfect blend of salt-and-pepper. The man's skin was smooth like rich cocoa, wrapped around chiseled features that told Francine that he was younger than the gray in his hair indicated. His eyes never left hers even when Garrison, noticing the intensity of the man, cleared his throat.

"Dr. Carty," the man said, his voice, a rumble Francine could have identified had the face not thrown her off.

But it was the smile that sealed the deal. The man's face lit up the room when he could tell that she was beginning to recognize him.

"Oh my God! Zech?!" Francine yelped as she leapt across the elevator to hug him.

Zech smiled again at Francine and then soberly looked back and forth between Francine, who'd suddenly felt panicked, and Garrison, whose face was twisted in confusion. Just then, the doors opened on Zech's floor and he stepped off the elevator.

"Wait … are you here for a conference?" Francine asked him.

Zech, feeling the weight of his emotions crushing him, answered quickly, "Yes, Francine. I'll be in touch."

And then he was gone.

Zech didn't know if what he'd said was true. Whether he'd really talk to Francine again. He didn't know if he could take one more heart-wrenching save. That was a pattern and role he was determined to not repeat. In fact, after the revelatory results of his last journey, he knew he could no longer play savior to anyone anymore. Not even for someone he loved.

"Who is that guy?" Garrison asked, back on the elevator.

Francine didn't answer him. Just like her meds, it was no longer his business.

But in her heart, she knew the answer.

15

Francine's mind was reeling. *Why hadn't Zech mentioned a conference in the States? He knew she was on her way back.*

By now, they were in Francine's room. Garrison munched on the colorful presentation of strawberries, grapes, and pineapple as he uncorked the bottle of champagne that chilled in a silver chrome bucket, leaving his gift of Riesling on ice. He passed her the card. It read:

Dr. Carty,

Thank you for joining us. Welcome home!

Board of Directors
The Sherman Fellowship

Francine kicked off her shoes and slipped her manicured feet into the complimentary apricot-colored slippers. Garrison handed her the glass of champagne.

"A toast. To the triumphant return of the lovely Dr. Francine Carty," his glass tinged hers.

"Thank you, Garrison," Francine said as she invited him to have a seat on the white leather sofa, a beautiful 19th century reproduction. She sat adjacent on a plush chaise lounge.

"You were amazing up there, Francine. And you look," he paused, "fantastic!" Placing his glass on the table, Garrison stood and walked toward her.

Shoot! She thought to herself. She was fine until he got too close. He sat close to her on the chaise. The familiar scent of his sweat and cologne awakened hard-fought memories. Francine arched her back, a gesture to disguise her body's response to his and to draw upon the formality she replayed in her imagined scenario of how this reunion would unfold.

He began with a heartfelt apology. Again. He admitted how selfish he had been in their relationship. And how he owed her more respect than he had shown. He confessed that he felt quite lost with her departure and the realization of what she had meant to him. And finally, that he still and would always love her.

Garrison said all the right things. Francine wanted and needed to hear him say them even after all of this time. She remained silent for a few beats.

Francine sat looking into Garrison's eyes.

"Thank you. I really needed to hear those words from you," she smiled, fighting back the emotion that was welling up. "I forgive you, Garrison. If I'm honest, I knew your heart was never fully mine. I just didn't want to admit it until I was left with no choice. I'll always love you, too. But things are different, Garrison. I've changed."

Before Francine could continue, Garrison cupped her face in his large hands and began kissing her. First her forehead, then her face, and finally his mouth met hers like a magnet. Francine forgot her practiced script only to realize it had been almost a year since she'd kissed a man intimately—well, at least while she was in her right mind. Her inhibitions evaporated. Her body succumbed to his. Garrison lay on top of her on the chaise. He undressed her as if he were a madman. His legs straddled her, one foot on the floor, one knee bent at the seam of the chaise lounge as he ripped open the buttons of his shirt and tie, revealing his laser cut arms and six-pack beneath the fitted undershirt. Francine did the honors of removing it.

He kissed her in all the meaningful places. His mouth watered to taste all of her.

"Your changes are magnificent," he said as he gripped her newly rounded out hips and bottom.

"That skirt was killing me," he panted, as he tore open the condom wrapper clenched between his teeth and rolled it on.

He moved his hands to caress her hair, "You're perfect, you know that? I love everything about you."

You're perfect.

His words triggered the anger Francine thought was long gone. The way he idealized the woman he betrayed her for. The woman he had always attempted to shape her into—his project, his pet. But the time away had restored Francine. She no longer needed the Garrisons of the world anymore—people who harped on her imperfections, instead of tending their own. The time she spent forgiving herself of her failings and listening to others' similar stories had empowered her to accept herself and others for who they are, not what they've done or accomplished. In that instant, her heart overrode her old habit, snuffing out her momentary jones.

"Garrison. This isn't me anymore. Please get up. I need you to go," Francine said resolutely.

Garrison stared at her first in disbelief, then in resignation, then finally, with a cruel smirk. "What, you need some cherries or something, now? I'll call down to the bar."

As quickly as the cruel words attempting to demean her spilled out, he began his apologies, "I didn't mean that. It was a bad joke. I didn't mean it. I'm sorry."

Francine was done. Without a word, she slid from under him and wrapped herself in the hotel robe that lay on the chair next to the chaise. She then gathered her clothing from the floor and placed them on the bed.

"I need a *shower*. Let yourself out," she looked him in the eye and this time he barely recognized her. "And don't come back."

Francine stepped into the lavish bathroom and locked the door. Her back against the door, her chest heaved with rage. She was angry with Garrison and with herself for allowing him back into her life, if only for a moment.

"Frankie. Frankie!" Garrison pleaded.

He quickly put on his underwear and walked over to the bathroom. He placed his hand on the outside of the door and whispered, his voice turned raw with emotion, "Goodbye, Frankie." Garrison collected himself, dressed, and left.

When Francine heard Garrison leave, she brushed her teeth as if scouring away any remnants of Garrison's kisses. She stepped into a long, steamy shower, then dressed for dinner with Ursula. She wondered if Zech was staying in the hotel. She called the front desk and asked for Dr. Zechariah Johns. As luck would have it, he was!

"I'll connect you, Dr. Carty," the desk clerk offered.

Francine's strength was renewed. She decided to be proud of herself for catching her descent into Garrison's lair instead of punishing herself for undoing her important progress.

No answer.

She had hoped he might join them for dinner or later. She really wanted her two good friends to finally meet in person. Her lamentation was interrupted by a knock at the door.

Her heart leapt hoping it might be Zech.

It was!

Francine felt an unexpected, refreshing joy—pure and consuming—seeing him standing before her.

"Zech. Get in here! I'm stunned. I just tried to call you. What are you doing here?"

Francine couldn't hide her confusion at his being at the conference and of course, his shearing of his entire head and face. She stared hard at him the entire time she leveled her inquiry. But she mostly caught only his profile. He stood in the doorway, never crossing the threshold.

"And look at you! M*y goodness*," she continued.

He shot a look in her direction, but his attention stood fast on something in the hallway.

"What's going on out there?" Francine leaned in close to Zech, who did not move, in order to poke her head out to get a view into the corridor.

"Jesus, help me …" she sighed.

It was Garrison.

Zech had been watching him approach all this time. The last thing Francine needed was another embarrassing performance. And Lord knows she could not afford to replace a single item in this suite. Maybe he was just here to apologize. Again. Maybe. But the look he wore as he recognized Zech as the man from the elevator, said otherwise.

"Garrison, what are you doing?" Francine now stood in the doorway with Zech.

"I'm here for you, Frankie." His eyes locked with Zech's for a moment, then he looked at her. "I don't know who this guy is, but you belong with me."

Belong?

"Garrison, you don't own me. I am not your lost little girl anymore," Francine calmly stated.

As she said the words, she could feel Zech's familiar smirk. She didn't dare turn to look at him. By the scowl that appeared on Garrison's face, she was correct about the smirk. Zech was moving from behind her now and stepped fully into the hallway.

A fight between these two men whom she loved in such different ways was the last thing she thought she'd experience today. She was glad Zech was here to witness her watershed moments: The presentation—had he actually seen it? And her standing up for herself with Garrison once and for all. He didn't necessarily need to know what occurred in the interim. *Wait, why do I care if he knows?* She checked herself.

Before Francine could process the rest of her thought, fists began to fly!

Garrison had pretended to walk away but turned quickly and threw a jab that landed square on Zech's jaw. *Not the smile!* Francine panicked. To her relief and surprise, Zech didn't go down. In a flash,

Zech returned with a nasty right hook to Garrison's eye. But how long would that last? Garrison was significantly younger and stronger … and meaner—something she'd learned an hour ago. The last thing she wanted was for Zech to get hurt. She had to do something! This was her fault. The door slammed behind her as she ran inside. She picked up a heavy vase from the sitting area of the suite. She flung open the door expecting the men to be wrestling or bleeding, but there was silence. One of the men lay in the hallway, unconscious. Francine placed the vase by his feet and kneeled down to check his pulse.

"Oh, Zech!" Francine kneeled down but quickly realized the man who had been knocked out cold was Garrison!

"Zech!?" she smiled to herself. "Well, I'll be damned." She looked down the hallway in each direction, but he was gone.

Francine stood, collected the vase, and sat on the bed in awe and disbelief. She did the only thing she could. Calmly, she picked up the phone and dialed the front desk.

"Cleanup, just outside of the VIP!"

***

Zech couldn't believe what just happened. How did he end up in a fight with that jackass? He thought through the events of the past few hours on the way to the airport: *I knew better than to stop up to see Francine before leaving.*

His plan was to slip in to her presentation, incognito, and slip out an hour later. He had given a presentation the day before at a National Institute of Health meeting in California and wanted to share the results of his research with her. She was the one person in his life who understood its significance and would be as excited as he was. Besides, he couldn't miss her moment in the sun. He had been so careful with her. He loved feeling her arms around him and her face against his back on his motorbike, but he taught her to ride anyway. He loved her appetite for all kinds of knowledge and often had to control himself fantasizing about what they might teach each other if he ever had the privilege of holding her in his arms. He often watched her from the distance in the fields and from the greenhouse. He loved the intention with which she cared for her family, friends, and others, and lately, herself. He cherished their porch time. The night allowed him to stare at her hair, her face, her rice and beans—to dream of a future with her without her seeing. He was ready to shave months before she left, but he wanted to make his move on her turf so she could be fully grounded in whatever she decided she wanted with him.

I'm so proud of her!

Zech marveled at her presentation. All he wanted to do was hold Francine to let her know he was there supporting and celebrating her.

I shouldn't have let seeing her with Garrison shake me, but she'd done so well to get past him.

Zech couldn't blame Garrison for trying. Francine could get under your skin. The thing that bothered him was Francine looked as if she was getting drawn back in hook, line, and sinker.

She knows better!

Zech couldn't help it. He couldn't stop thinking about what could have been happening up in her room.

Francine is a grown woman. I should have called. What was I thinking just showing up at her door?

Sure, Zech wanted a glimpse of the infamous Garrison but a fight? Zech shook his head. What is it with him and damsels in distress?

Francine doesn't need me to save her. She is capable of handling her business.

Zech paid the cab driver, then handed off his bag to the skycap. Zechariah might have retired his superhero cape, but he was still committed to truth. He stood inside as the cool of the terminal's air conditioning snapped clear the haze in his mind. Instead of heading straight to the security check-in, he walked up to the ticket agent and stood there, decidedly.

The attendant, an attractive fortysomething woman with impeccably applied makeup, smiled at the tall, handsome man who stood before her. He looked exasperated, as if he had seen some tough times but better for the wear.

"Good afternoon, Sir. How may I help you?" she overtly flirted with Zech.

Flushed, he handed her his identification and credit card, "Good afternoon."

"Dr. Zechariah Johns. What can I do for you today?" she said, quasi-professionally

"Ma'am, I just need an open ticket," he said. "One way."

Zech forgot how forward women were with him when he actually showed himself. He was aware of his good looks but never was one for vanity. On the rare occasions he chose to clean up, he'd often forget that people weren't seeing the mountain man visage that usually served as an effective repellant.

"Oh, you're ma'am-ing me, huh," the attendant said as her fingers tapped the keyboard, "Your gray doesn't fool me. I know what 40 looks like. I've *been* 40."

Zech had to smile. The woman was the first in a long time to call him out for hiding behind his prematurely gray hair.

"Plus, that *smile*. Teeth don't lie, Dr. Johns!" she winked at him.

This time they shared a laugh. The attendant handed him the ticket, his impulse fulfilled.

"Good luck, Dr. Zechariah Johns," the attendant said looking him in the eye.

Recalling Francine's presentation and his visceral reaction to seeing her with Garrison, and now the age outing by the airline attendant, Zech begged the question, *What's with all the transparency today!?*

Reading her nametag, he bid her adieu, "Thank you, Vanessa."

***

Ursula waited for Francine in the lobby. She wore a strikingly sophisticated belted pantsuit.

"Wow, look at you!" Francine smiled. "Ivory is your color, girl!"

"Color us the mutual admiration society! You look lovely as well. You are killing me in these beautiful dresses. We are about the same size now, so I might have to borrow one from time to time," Ursula bumped Francine's hip with hers as the friends shared a laugh.

"Well, I have a surprise for you, so pull yourself together," Ursula said coyly.

Francine stopped dead in her tracks, "Please tell me you didn't invite Garrison."

"Hells, no. I've lost weight, not my mind!" Ursula whispered as they linked arms and walked toward the hotel restaurant.

"That's a relief, because he showed his …" Francine stopped at the most beautiful sight.

A chorus of, "*Frankieeeee*!!!" rang from a corner table. The entire Carty clan stood to greet her, applauding. Ursula clasped her hands with satisfaction from seeing her friend so happy. Frankie took turns hugging her family one by one. Ursula arranged for the waiter to bring lots of water and to give them a good 10 minutes before approaching the table. Her parents beamed with pride over the courage and grace their daughter displayed during her presentation--which they deliberately observed from the back row. Robbi complimented her baby sister on her fortitude, her eyes full with affirmation. Mrs. Carty clasped Ursula's hand across the table, thanking her for being such good friend to Francine.

Hours slipped by as they filled in the blanks left by the miles between them.

Toward the end of the evening, Mrs. Carty asked, "So where's this Dr. Zechariah Johns. I halfway expected to see him here."

Robbi popped a cube of ice in her mouth, with an expression that said, *Mmm hmmm.* Francine looked to her father, who wiped his mouth, and dropped the cloth napkin onto his plate with a look that said, *Well?*, his second to her mother's question.

Ursula leaned in as if to say, *Spill it, Girl!*

Francine used a move on them that would have made Zech proud.

Silence.

Only Mama Carty was not affected, the intention in her eyes intact.

"Actually," Francine began and they waited … also in silence, "he *is* here. Or was here. I don't know."

As Francine recounted the discovery that unfolded in the elevator, offering a G-rated version of the Garrison reunion and a thick description of the dramatic scene in the hallway, everyone's jaws dropped.

They responded all at once:

Robbi declared very officially, "I like him," and relaxed into her seat.

Ursula followed suit, "knocked 'im out cold, huh?" She smirked, relishing the image as if it were better than the scoop of raspberry sorbet she was licking from her dessert spoon.

"Well, when do we meet him?" Mr. Carty asked in expectation, though Francine knew her dad was a quiet storm, more angry now about Garrison than interested in the big reveal of Zech.

Francine broke the string of inquiry, "Look, he's a really good *friend*, not my *fiancé."*

Francine's mother looked into her daughter's eyes. Francine looked away.

"Francine, look at me" her mother said gently. "I knew you before you knew yourself. When we talked on the phone that day, I knew you were in love with that man, even if you didn't—even if you don't. Now, I wouldn't normally say this out in the open, but we are all family here.

Mr. Carty and Robbi smiled at Ursula then returned their eyes to the action.

"And seems to me, he loves you too," she held Francine's hand.

Her father added, "Listen, Baby girl. Sensible men don't take to fisticuffs … and shovels … for women they don't intend to honor."

"Benjamin!" Mrs. Carty said surprised by his inference.

Robbi mouthed to Francine, *"Shovels?"*

"I'll fill you in later," Frankie mouthed in reply.

Ursula just shook her head. "Knocked him out *COLD*."

The waiter appeared to inform Francine that *all* of her meals and gratuities in the hotel were included as part of the sponsorship of her stay by the Sherman Board.

"Well, looks as if we have two big shots in the family!" her father's chest swelled. "These Sherman people are a class act to the very end. I can't even treat my baby girl to a welcome back dinner."

Everyone stood up and leisurely head toward the hotel exit. They gave their last round of hugs and said goodbyes as they stood in front of the building facing 17th Street.

"We need to be on site tomorrow, there's a big funeral. But please know we're very proud of you!" her father said as he generously tipped the valet and got into their car.

Francine, Robbi, and Ursula waved goodbye.

Robbi was in the States for three weeks with time to burn, so she, Ursula, and Francine decided to spend the night at the suite to get caught up on the uncut versions of all that had transpired in the past several months. Ursula had shared a bit about a bourgeoning love affair and Robbi had an international lover of her own … plus there was work gab.

"I need to stop at the front desk, you all go ahead," Francine briskly walked to the lobby desk in hopes that there was a message from Zech.

Nothing.

Heading back to her room, she physically shook her hands in effort to shake off the disappointment she didn't fully understand.

What was she doing? She wasn't sure why her parents couldn't understand that her relationship with Zech wasn't a romantic one. She also couldn't deny how drop-dead gorgeous he was. She had always been drawn to him, his spirit, his honesty, his contemplative nature, his off-handed nurturing way with her. And she accepted his wilderness mindset as a complement to his appearance. Handling Garrison the way he did, she was afraid he would get hurt, but upon reflection, he spent hours tending those herbs and managing everything else around the farm. Why had she assumed he couldn't handle himself? Then again, the hair, the beard, and those overalls covered up a lot. Was he hiding? If so, why was he revealing himself now? Francine answered her own question. *He did say he only groomed his hair when he traveled internationally and he might be clean-shaven the next time we saw each other.*

Francine was in such despair during her first weeks at the farm. She'd ridden on the back of the motorbike, but she didn't remember the firm fitness that the dark tailored suit implied that afternoon. How *old* was he anyway? She always guessed he was somewhere around his early 60s but well preserved. But the man she saw today shaved a good 20 years off her estimate. What was she doing? This was *Zech*! Surely she would have known if he were only a few years her senior. She tried to reevaluate his connection to Adjowa with the new age in range. Had she dropped any breadcrumbs? Shoot, did she even know?

Ding! The elevator chimed, and the doors opened to her floor. Inside her room, Robbi and Ursula were seated outside on the balcony. Francine needed a minute. She changed into yoga pants and a tank top and sat on the edge of the bed. Out of the corner of her eye, she noticed an envelope with her name on it. In the upper corner, the hotel insignia and address appeared.

She opened it. Inside was a small padded envelope. It read:

I found it.

The handwriting was familiar. She opened the envelope. Inside was a small vial with a label marked *Susu.*

16

Francine's mind raced as she slammed the trunk of her rental closed. The car, a small crossover SUV, was packed with mostly clothes, shoes, and books. She'd shipped ahead several boxes of her belonging, but for the most part, everything else she'd owned—furniture and other effects—were either staying with Ursula, sold to the Temple University graduate student she'd found on Craigslist, or being given away to the Whosoever Gospel Mission's thrift shop over on Chelten Avenue. She'd officially pared down her life—something she would have never dreamed of doing had she not seen firsthand the peace that can come from living simply and purposefully. Francine would always thank Zech for the many lessons she learned during her time with him.

Zech.

What could she say? He was gone. Two weeks of trying to reach out to him had been fruitless. She'd even gone as far as contacting the transportation center near the farm where he picked up his mail.

"Ahhh, Professor Zech's Frankieee!" the man said, drawing out the vowels.

He remembers me! The acknowledgement and association with Zech made Francine hopeful. Her hopes, though, were soon dashed.

"No, Sister. The doctor has not been here in quite some time. I believe he is traveling. If you do speak with him, please let him know that he has plenty of correspondence here."

Francine assured the man that she would pass along the message if she spoke to Zech. The chances of that seemed slim.

Snap! Snap!

"Uhhh. Hellooooo?!"

Ursula stood in front of Francine, next to the car, snapping her fingers and trying to bring her back from her mental playback.

"Where are you, girl? You seem out of it. Are you going to be okay to drive?"

Francine returned to the present and smiled at her friend.

"I'm fine."

Ursula wasn't convinced but decided to leave Frankie to her thoughts. She suspected rightly that Francine's mind was still fixed on a certain American expatriate in Ghana.

"So, listen. The house is yours for as long as you need it. My family hasn't used the cottage in ages. I've had the caretaker prepare it for you so it should be ready to enjoy."

Ursula handed a set of keys to Francine who had tears threatening to fall from her eyes.

"I don't know how to thank you, Ursula. I never thought I'd be leaving Philly and Ravencrest. At least not so soon."

"Well ummm, ma'am. Between your presentation going viral, invitation to TED, publishers circling like sharks, and now the teaching gig at UVA, I'd say that the timing is absolutely perfect."

Francine shrugged. "I guess you're right."

Ursula took her friend's hands in her own. The simple gesture of love and sisterhood broke the dam in Francine and her tears began to fall freely.

"I know I'm right. Spend some time with your family in Maryland. Go to Virginia. Rest your mind …" Ursula looked at Francine knowingly, "…and your heart. Write that book and continue your conversations with sisters all around this country who need to be set free by your story. But most of all, take some time out for yourself and prepare for your next move."

Francine smiled through the tears. "Or rather God's next move. Because who would have ever thought …"

Ursula nodded her head but interrupted, "Frankie, you're amazing. Go be amazing."

With that, Francine hugged Ursula tightly and got into the car. As she pulled off, Francine waved to her friend who she was sure she'd see many times again. She also waved goodbye to a life that was surely gone forever.

***

The St. James cottage was everything Francine needed but "cottage" was beyond an understatement. What Ursula called "The Cottage" was actually a six-bedroom, four-bath, 19th century farmhouse sitting on 30 acres of land. The gardens around the home were landscaped to perfection with large purple-fringed orchids and yellow star grass growing wild further out on the property. *Zech would love this place,* the thought stole into Francine's head. There was a luxurious pool and hot tub that sat just off of an elaborately landscaped stone patio behind the home.

It was, in short, Francine's corner of heaven. In the three weeks since she first pulled up in front of the home, she'd traveled quite a bit and stayed in some magnificent hotels and B&Bs. But it was St. James Place, as she'd taken to calling it, that became her sanctuary.

***

"It was all a dream, I used to read Word Up magazine ..."

Francine reached out from the thick, lush bedcover and grabbed her cell phone to turn off her "Biggie alarm." When her eyes adjusted to the light streaming into her room, she focused on the phone's screen. 11:07. She sighed.

"If I'm ever going to finish this book, I need to get up much earlier," she mumbled aloud to herself.

The birds that often perched outside the large plantation shuttered picture window responded with tweets and chirps. She yawned, stretched, and inhaled the fresh air.

Francine got out of bed and began her routine. Warm shower. Robe on. Head straight to the kitchen. Put on some tea. Take tea and laptop to the back patio. Check her social networks. Scroll through her favorite blogs. And …

Francine's finger stopped on a headline that caused her to swallow her hot tea a little too quickly, slightly burning her tongue and throat.

Socialite, Patrice Lashley, to Wed Longtime Beau

The picture of Garrison and Patrice smiling back at her stunned Francine. She couldn't believe her eyes, and then again, she totally could. And though it stung more than a little bit, Francine wasn't distraught about the announcement. Garrison was her past, and he ultimately wanted something from her, wanted her to be something that she never wanted to be. She lifted her mug of tea in the air, nodded her head, and said, "Salud, Garrison." She then poured a little of the tea out onto the patio as a libation.

As Francine swiped her finger across the screen to read the next post, she heard the front doorbell ring. She was slightly perplexed by the intrusion as she rarely had any visitors and certainly not so early in the day.

Must be a delivery guy, she thought as she walked barefoot—a habit she picked up in Ghana—through the large galley kitchen, formal dining room, hanging a left to the front door. When she peeked through the keyhole, her mouth dropped open in surprise. She quickly tied her robe and opened the door.

"JOSEPH!"

Francine hugged her old friend and driver whose eyes were lit with joy; his smile was wide with happiness. He was wearing linen slacks and a short-sleeved shirt made of traditional fabric. She recognized the design from Judith's inventory.

"So nice to see you, Mme. Carty!"

"Oh my God! What in the world are you doing here? How did you find me? Welcome! Welcome!" Francine shrieked using the greeting she had become accustomed to in Accra.

Joseph held up his hand to stop her avalanche of words.

“What?!” Francine said.

Joseph stepped aside to reveal the real reason for showing up on her doorstep.

Leaning against a big-bodied F150 pick-up truck, dressed in cream linen pants and a turquoise shirt that accentuated the dip and curve of every muscle as well as a narrow waist, was Zechariah Johns. Francine half-heartedly wished for the safety of the old overalls, but that smile, it gave her all the stability she needed. His smile was like the morning sun drawing out a flower to bloom. Francine ran past Joseph and right into Zech’s arms. The completion of her own Susu journey had come.

In that moment, Francine and Zech spoke to each other in a language that had become so familiar to them.

Silence.

Epilogue

The young woman was obviously anxious. She held her hands to keep them from shaking. Her voice quaked ever so slightly when she spoke. But she certainly looked the part. She was impeccably dressed. Her hair, pulled back in a tasteful, intricately braided bun. Makeup wasn't overdone but enhanced her rich, dark complexion and bright, almond eyes.

Most of all, she was brilliant. Of course, she didn't really know that. That's how most of them come in. The women had been watching this one for quite some time. Engaging her students in her lectures. Writing profound think pieces for some of the most selective academic journals and commercial publications. But, yes, slightly awkward. She was going to need some work as far as her confidence. Her social skills. But that was never a deal breaker when it came to The Search's selection process. The Search always looked for a certain kind of woman. One that exuded inner strength and resilience. Being a successful woman of color and part of the exclusive network was not for the faint of heart. It took more than intelligence and drive. It took the ability to empower and be empowered. One had to be great.

This one certainly had the potential to be great, but there would be a number of tests she'd have to overcome, a number of risks she'd have to be willing to take, in order for the committee to know for sure. She likely thinks that her acceptance for The Search Fellowship will simply come by post or email. Oh, if it were only that easy!

The assistant delivers the woman into the boardroom and asks her to sit in a chair at the head of a long teak wood table. Seated around the formal tea setting are four women: Dr. Roseline Mercer, Mme. Fosua Addo, the proxy for Dr. Charlotte Botchwey, and the director of the program who smiled warmly at the young woman.

"Good Afternoon, Ms. Esi Mensah. As discussed in our initial meeting, I, Dr. Francine Carty-Johns, will be facilitating our conversation today."

THE END

About the Authors

T.M. Giggetts

As a writer, editor, educator, and entrepreneur, T.M. Giggetts offers those who hear her speak and read her work an authentic experience—an opportunity to explore the intersection of identity (race, class, and culture), faith, and purpose at the deepest levels. She holds a Bachelor of Arts degree in communication from the University of Kentucky, an M.B.A. degree in marketing from Montclair State University in New Jersey, and an M.F.A in creative writing from Fairleigh Dickinson University. The author of eight books across multiple genres, Giggetts has been published in local, regional, and national print and online publications, including TheRoot.com, Ebony.com, Dame Magazine, The Chronicle for Higher Education, MyBrownBaby.com, xoJane.com, and more. This Louisville, KY, native currently resides in the metro Philadelphia with her husband and daughter.

Marcella McCoy-Deh

Marcella McCoy-Deh, PhD, enjoys writing children's literature, adult fiction, and essays. She teaches courses in history, social science, and writing and enjoys international and domestic travel. McCoy-Deh, who lives in Philadelphia with her husband and daughter, is an academic administrator and professor at Philadelphia University. The Philadelphia native is an alumna of Morgan State University in Maryland and Bowling Green State University in Ohio. She has also lived in the Hampton Roads area of Virginia. She has been previously published as an academic, a journalist, and a magazine contributor. *The Search for Susu* is McCoy-Deh's first novel.

About NewSeason Books

NewSeason Books is an independent publisher of transformational literature—boundary-breaking books. We are committed to providing quality content and stories that assist people in growing personally and spiritually. Visit us online!

www.newseasonbooks.com
FB: facebook.com/newseasonbooks
Twitter: @newseasonbooks

Have you ever been humiliated (online or in real life) for something you've done or were involved in? How were you able to overcome the shame and rejection that came along with that?

Go to the "The Search for Susu Readers" Facebook group to share your thoughts! Like Francine Carty, there's freedom in sharing your story on your own terms!

We'd love to hear from you!

Tracey & Marcella